For more information go to RobertsBooks.com
Or – Amazon.com Keyword: "Roberts Pupperteer"

Roberts Books ID#   SOLO-004001STS-0002

ISBN - 978-1-475-14364-5

Thank you

To my wife

It's all for you baby. It's always been
for you.

The Puppeteer

Book 1

By

Michael
Roberts

Narrated by

Jason Pinc

Note from the Author

This story is my life. I have changed a few things to keep my family and friends safe. The characteristics revolving around me and my personality are all true.

I wrote this little book, I am told it is called a novella, because my therapist thinks I need an "outlet" after what happened. What better way than to tell my story?

Ok, I am not a writer; I don't have the luxury of an editor or thousands of dollars to get this professionally proofed. I am a police officer and we really don't make that much.

Picture my book like this: You are sitting in your favorite reading spot. If you are not, I ask you to go there. A big couch, a bay window, or a comfy chair with dog bite marks on it. Where ever it is, sit there and read. I don't know how to write other than like I am telling you the story.

So that is how it will be. I am going to write as if I am in the room with you telling my story. Picture me sitting on the couch or chair or leaning against the wall stressing about the events I am telling you.

I may break from my story and talk to you directly, to tell you a little bit about myself. Please do not worry I will go back to the story and finish.

Like I said, most of this is based on real events, a lot of it has been changed to protect myself and others, and to keep "confidential" information just that.

Some of the officers in this are described to the best of my knowledge. Some may come across as "Dicks" and some cops are. But you have to keep in mind that they put there life on the line every day and they are really stressed out. Several are struggling to make ends meet.

If I have one thing to ask is that, if possible, respect them around you. Donate your time and money, if possible, to your local PD. Trust me they need it.

Thank you for reading my little snippet. I really hope you find this book entertaining.

- Jayson Pinc

Chapter 1

It was always hard for me to get to sleep. I don't understand why. It just seemed to come so easily for my wife, Sidney.

My world revolved around something most people don't even realize they are looking at. The clocks, the so many, many clocks I've seen in any given day. They all laughed at me, they did, they always told me what time it was and screamed the fact that I was not sleeping… still.

I looked up at the ceiling… again. I did whatever I could to get my mind off of the fact that the clock was shining in my eyes.

"4:17am."

It had to remind me that yes; I would be getting up in less than an hour.

Our ceiling was that cheap spray on insulation they put in crappy apartments in New York. It was white and bumpy casting thousands of shadows. Faces, pictures, and diagrams of things that were, and were to be, showed up in the shadows. Maybe it was the lack of sleep. I tried to count them a few times to get to sleep but nothing seemed to help.

Our apartment was a small place but it was all ours. In twenty-seven more payments it would be all ours.

"4:18am." It has been only one minute. I guess I should just get up and get a start on the day.

I tossed the thick blanket off my body and sat up. I was wearing my normal sleeping getup, the bright red pajama pants and a black t-shirt.

I rubbed my eyes, not like they were sleepy or anything, just habit. I kept telling Sidney that I was sleeping just fine. I didn't want her to worry.

She worries about everything, from problems with her to her family to her job. But most of all… me. Who could blame her really?

She hasn't even asked me about it in the last few months, but that isn't her fault I guess. She must have gotten tired of me lying to her. She had to know I wasn't sleeping well. The bags under my eyes alone could tip someone off. I was only twenty-seven at the time and having trouble sleeping already. I wondered what great things I had in store for me later in life.

I clicked the alarm to 'off' and got up. I walked the few feet to the door and turned around. My wife was such a sound sleeper... must be nice. Her dark brown hair, or whatever color it was this month, laid on the light blue pillow. I thought to myself, "How did I ever get so lucky?"

She was so pretty. It was strange that she would ever wind up with a broke, weird looking guy like me. But I was not complaining. No, no I was not. I was happy.

I opened my dresser and every single time I saw it I jumped a little.

The matte black pistol, resting from the night before, on top of my socks and underwear. I pick it up and bring it to the bathroom with me. I never did like guns but what can I say, it is a requirement being an officer of the law.

I carry it wherever I go, yes, even to the bathroom. It had its own small ledge to sit on while I showered. I built it when we moved in just over, four years ago now.

That reminds me...

I got my first gun when I was eleven; my father got me a BB-gun. Okay, okay. It may not have been a real gun but I felt like the toughest guy on the block. I was too, ask anyone. I was the greatest. My father was an officer too, a detective actually. I still remember how he gave it to me...

It was my eleventh birthday. We lived in a small house in suburbia, an hour or so, east of New York. We never did have a lot of money.

My father was a cop. And my mother only worked thirty-eight hours a week at a convenience store.

"Cheap bastard."

The owner only had her work thirty-eight instead of forty so he didn't have to pay her benefits.

That is for another time.

But every year I was so happy to have anything, anything at all that I was never disappointed with my presents.

My father, the trickster he was, gave me a box covered in wrapping paper. I tore it open with excitement looking inside the plain brown box. A smile crept over my face. The countless possibilities that could lie inside, teased my mind. I ripped open the box with vigorous intensity, at the bottom, there sat a package of BB pellets. I simply looked up confused holding the small cylinder in between my thumb and pointer finger.

My dad said, "It's for your BB-gun."

My dad forgot a lot of stuff in his days... another great thing I get to look forward to when I get older. I smiled and told him that I did not have one but I could do something else with them.

My dad thinking that I had ruined his perfectly good joke asked me what I was talking about.

I stood up and walked casually to the silverware drawer and pulled out a spoon.

My father smiled and looked at me with anticipation. Wondering what I was going to possibly do with a spoon and a BB.

I put one BB on the spoon and pulled the cup back and flung it across the room and hit him right in the eye. He hunched over grabbing at his eye, groaning. Then the most beautiful sound an eleven-year-old could ever hear. He could not stop laughing.

He pointed to the corner and told my mom to "Give it to me." She got up and grabbed a long box covered in shimmering paper from the closet. My father had one hand on his eye, applying pressure to his now swelling face. His other eye watched every movement I was making. His smile would be something I could not ever forget.

I ripped off the paper and tossed it in the air in little pieces, confetti rained all over the kitchen. My heart was pounding; I could not remember being this happy, excited, blessed. Call it what you will, I was grinning ear to ear. I opened the box and I pulled out a brand new bb-gun. It was never owned by anyone else, it was all mine. The tape across the box was not cut or re-masked. It was new! New, new, it really was the greatest birthday ever.

I would never forget that birthday, the year I knew without a shadow of a doubt. I wanted to be just like my dad.

I got out of the shower, grabbed my towel and dried off. It was tight quarters in the bathroom, the small sink and the shower and toilet filled 99.9% of the room. The other 0.1% was filled with me. Yeah, it was tight.

It made every activity one that would take half as long in a bigger room. But like the BB-gun, it one day would be all mine.

I never wanted lots of money or fancy things. All I wanted was love, I had it, and all I wanted in the whole world was asleep in the next room.

After my shower I walked into my bedroom. I never took cloths with me; not enough room. It was always freeing to walk down my own hallway naked. We had windows everywhere and neighbors just about every which way, and they were only feet from us. I never really cared, if they wanted to look then go ahead. Look.

I turned the corner into my room, it was still very dark out and my wife was snoring again, even though most people don't like that sound, I don't think there could be anything cuter. I sat and watched her breathe for a little bit. The blanket above her rising and falling with every breath, she was a miracle, my little miracle.

After who knows how long I watched her sleep, I turned on the light in the closet, and looked at my dark blue uniform. I sighed, hoping one day they will finally promote me to detective.

I had solved a few cases but I was never acknowledged for my assistance. "To low on the totem poll" but I never did this for the money. I just want the street to be cleaner than the day before. Was that too much to ask?

I have a way of seeing things that most people don't. There is some mental disease that I have; if I remember correctly it is called, low latent inhibition.

Don't worry I'll get into that later.

Let's just say, no one ever wants to play chess with me. I was always very smart in school, my teachers all told me I should go into engineering or something but all I wanted to do is go straight into the academy, so here I am.

After I got dressed I walked out to the kitchen "slash" dinning room "slash" pantry. I squeezed myself in and sat down at my table. The small round table that was inches away form my refrigerator and sink and cabinets and everything else. It pretty much filled most of the room. But, I was always happy.

I would not turn down a million dollars if someone gave it to me, but the most valuable thing I could think of was snoring in the room down the hall. I could not stop smiling the rest of my generic breakfast.

At 6:22 every morning I walked into the bedroom after the shower, the food, and the paper. I bent over and kissed Sidney on the forehead. I left the bedroom looking back at her one last time, and walked to the front door.

I looked in the mirror, just as I was about to walk out. Like every morning I read my name badge, "Officer J. Pinc" and read the note perfectly in place next to it. It was written by my wife when we first got married and I took this job. The note said, "'Officer J. Pinc' will be returning home under his own power at 6:45pm."

I liked my last name, it was Pinc, but it sounded like the color "pink." It was Nordic or something. I liked the name but I hated when I was called "Pinky." My friends did it to me a lot.

I kissed my fingers and slapped the mirror as I walked out. Turned around and locked my door and all three deadbolts. I made the locks all the same so we only need one key. However, I decided I was going to mess with anyone who would want to brake in. I turned the deadbolt around so the key had to be put in backward. I put a gear inside that turned the cylinder right way.

It was just a little thing I liked to do, tinker.

The hallway was narrow and dark. The one window in the hallway was probably cleaned in 1934 and then never again. It was covered in dust from when the building was made. Let's just say, not a whole lot of light came in through it. The walls were brown and drab, from dust, lack of light, and other "non-kosher" things to talk about.

I turned and started to walk down the steps, there were twelve in each set. On the third floor, the one I lived on, I grabbed the loose side rail and wiggled it. I could have fixed it years ago, but I did it on my first day and I will do it every day to give me good luck.

After the next two flights of stairs I opened the main door to my building. The broken shatter-proof glass made the outside world seem like a dream. I turned the handle at exactly 6:34am every morning to see the sun just breaking over some of the buildings in the distance and it showed the briefest moment of heaven. I breathed deeply and turned right to head to work.

* * *

My desk was small and filled to the rafters with papers and little gadgets and gizmo's I have built over the years. A picture of Sidney and I was sitting on the corner. It was the only proof that I had some kind of order in my life. The chaos on my desk said otherwise.

I loved how Sidney looked in pictures, if only she liked getting them taken more. I hated how I looked too. But who doesn't.

I was about six foot two and weighed two hundred and five pounds. My dark blond hair was thinning and blended in a "little too nicely" with the backdrop. A real bummer but I could get over it. I did have glasses for a long time, but doctors told me I didn't need them anymore so my face seemed empty to people who knew me. I think they will get used to it but for the time being I will live with the strange looks every time my friends see me.

I could not believe how pasty I looked, all the time. "Man, I am one ugly dude." I said quietly to myself.

My jaw had been broken once before so I had a nice chiseled chin and some would say I have a cute face, but I don't want to be cute. I am an officer, I want to be sexy... that will never happen.

My wife... now she was sexy. Her beautiful green eyes and her perfectly silky hair was long. It reached just below her shoulders. Her lips were smooth and her skin perfect. She could have been a model if she wanted to, but this was New York and she hated the typical "Blond bimbos" that walked the streets wherever we went. She said all the time she would not want to be one.

"C'est la vie." I said aloud again. I talk to myself a lot who doesn't?

"Pinc!"

"Sir!" as I stood as straight as I could. I turned around to hard laughing. "Dang it! Vince. Why do you do that?"

"Because, it's funny every time." He said. "You always want to impress but you will never be seen down here. We are gophers you know this."

"Some day I will work my way up. Some day I will. Mark my words and I'll remember who my friends are." I looked at him with tight eyes.

"Okay, okay, I give. I won't do it anymore." Vince said as he sat down at his own desk. That was, believe it or not, dirtier than mine. "So are you still going to get more pictures with Sidney tomorrow at the mall?"

"Yeah I don't wear glasses anymore and her hair is much longer now." I said, but never looked up from the picture in my hands.

"Pinc!" Instinctively, I thought it was Vince. Then a loud cough and I looked at him. His face was red and he was looking beyond my shoulders.

I could feel there was someone behind me and I could not stand up. My legs were frozen. Did I just blow it? Oh God help me. Move stupid! Move!

I shot up and turned around, Lieutenant Richards was standing at my desk and tapping his foot. "Lieutenant Richards... I uh-"

"Save it. My office. Five minutes." His face was flat and impatient.

I looked down at the ground and said, "Yes sir."

I stand and say "Sir" for three years and I blow it when it is real.

Vince was giggling and pointing.

"Dick!" I shouted as I walked past his desk and punched him in the arm. He laughed out loud and smiled. He didn't notice but, I looked back at him as he was rubbing his shoulder.

I had gotten much stronger over the years, an hour and a half in the gym every day after work made me one of the strongest in my section... most were nerds like me, but still, it was nice.

I got to the Lieutenant's office and stood at the ready. I don't think I have ever been this scared.

He spoke to his desk as he was writing something down, "You have been here for how many years?"

I was so excited I could barley speak, "F...f... four years now."

"And you have taken the detective exam and passed with-" He shuffled through his papers, "Wow one hundred percent. You think you are some kind of genius?"

"Ye-" I stopped myself. "No sir, just happy to be part of the team."

"Be honest, I know that you are a smart guy. You probably could be working for the military or something but you wanted to work here. Why?"

"My father was a detective and I looked up to him and wanted to be just like him."

"You speak of him in the past tense. Has he... past?"

"No sir, just-" Could I tell him, "retired."

"Good to hear. Anyway, I called you in here to tell you, that I would love for you to be on the detective team."

A smile the size of the Grand Canyon took over my face.

"However!"

Good feeling gone.

"We are stretched as thin as we can, we do not have a place for you. But I will tell you as soon as there is an opening. You will be my first choice. Do we have a deal?"

The smile was smaller but I was still so happy. "Yes sir." I put out my hand and waited for him to look up from what he was doing. He never did.

"You may go now, Pinc."

I put my hand awkwardly back into my pocket and said, "Thank you, sir." I turned and left in haste. Off to tell Vince the good news.

Chapter 2

The day was normal, slow. I did a patrol from 1:00 to 3:30. There was nothing really. I stopped a person from stealing, a petty crime. It was some fat kid, stealing some candy and chips. He was fifteen, white, about four-four and about one hundred and ten pounds.

I pressed the solid wooden black baton to his neck and told him that if I ever saw him stealing again that he would face me 'off the clock'.

His face turned whiter than my pasty face. I held back a giggle. He nodded and then took off running. Probably the most exercise he has gotten in years.

Vince never did understand why I did that. It was not up to him, but I wanted cleaner streets not to have a dirty cell back at the station. And he would learn his lesson and I hoped straighten out and become a contributing person in society.

We stopped at this small diner that we stopped at as often as possible. The coffee was down right terrible but the home made jam... amazing. I have a huge weakness for jam.

I stepped in and the waitress waved to me and pointed to an empty booth. She was cute; she was about five foot nothing and weighted only one hundred pounds. She has blond curly hair and a faint tint of red peeked from her roots.

"How are you fine officers doing on this sunny summer day?" She said perky as ever.

"Dina, when are you just going to say 'Hi Jay. Hi Vince. Good to see you again?'"

"When you are not officers, I have the most respect for the men in blue."

"Yeah you do." Vince said looking her up and down. He hit on her nearly every day. She worked all the time and Vince was there for, what I could assume, was not the jam.

"You... don't drink your coffee." Dina said as she stepped away. Her face and tone was like ice, cold and hard.

"Why? Are you going to spit in it? It might make it taste better." Again he looked her up and down. He was just a horny, lonely man. I chuckled to myself, but that was me once. I, at one point in time, did not have a wife who loved me. She was just a woman I worked with at some crappy retail job. Again, it's a story for another time.

"Why do you think yours tastes so bad?" She said as she smiled and winked at me.

"What?" Vince looked like he was about to puke.

"She is just kidding... you pervert. Leave her alone."

Vince ate his toast and slowly sipped at his coffee. His hands shook as he took each sip, examining every drop.

After the toast Dina brought the check and I reached for it. Vince snatched it out of my hands before I realized it. He said, "No, no, no. This one is on me. We are celebrating, Mister... almost detective."

"Woo! I saved like three bucks-" I said sarcastically, "and please, don't call me that."

He paid the bill and we walked back to the station.

We got back at 3:37 and reported in. The rest of the day I was sitting at my desk working on the latest gizmo I was making.

"What is this one?" Vince said as he saw me tinkering.

"It's a key lo-jack."

"What? You're putting a GPS on your keys?"

"Why not, I lose them all the time. I think Sidney would like one. Would you?"

"No man, I am good. I don't need a five pound object hanging from my keys."

I could not stop laughing. "It will weigh about an ounce once it's done."

"Maybe." He got up to go get some REAL coffee.

* * *

At the end of the work day I was finished with Sidney's lo-jack. It was a small metal box about a quarter of an inch thick and an inch wide and an inch long.

"Lets see if it works." I said as I toggled the little switch inside and closed it up with a small little screw. I tossed it to Vince. "Go hide it somewhere in the station."

Nearly ten minutes later he came back with a smile on his face. "You will never find that thing Pinky, EVER!" I hated it, that he called me pinky.

I logged onto my phone and went to a website I built a few months ago for these objects. I plugged in the serial number '042506001'. It was our anniversary and then 'zero- zero- one' to show the number. I always thought about Sidney even when tinkering. Plugged in the password and "ding!" the screen came to life.

Sure enough on my phone popped up a little blinking red dot that was nearly on top of me. I zoomed in and it said it was down the hall.

I followed the blinking dot on my screen until I was standing in front of the ladies room. I turned around and saw Vince bending over laughing as he pointed at me. I pushed open the door and said, "Hello? Officer Pinc!" I was trying to announce myself and I walked in. Two female officers were in there looking into the mirror.

My face was never redder. I asked them if I could look around and see if I could find a small metal object. They looked at me like I was from mars. But they said, "Knock yourself out." and waved me on.

I pulled up my phone and followed the dot till it pointed me to the taller of the two. It was on her. Dang it Vince!

"Miss I am so sorry but I think that my friend may have planted a bug on you. Can you check your pockets and purse?"

"Sure." She said with a shrug of her shoulders. She emptied her pockets and sure enough it was lodged in her back pocket. She held it out and dangled it in front of me.

She waved it back and forth and I reached for it. She quickly pulled it away. You have to pay for it.

I reached into my wallet and grabbed a twenty. Handing it to her I thought, "I just paid for my own object back." She dropped it into my hand

"I would have accepted a phone number."

"I am sorry, but I am married." I said as I twirled the ring on my left hand.

"Why are the cute ones always taken? I will keep and eye out for you, sugar. Let me know if it all works out." She winked and walked out of the bathroom.

I gripped the device in my hand and was red with the fire burning for Vince. I am going to punch him so hard; his head will be in another time zone.

* * *

I got back home after the gym at 6:45 on the dot. I love it when it all works out. A wonderful aroma settled into my nose as I locked the door behind me. Sidney was such a good cook. She made home made meals whenever she could. She worked as a secretary at a small family owned medical office and was home at 4:00pm every day. She went out and started to make dinner so it would be ready by the time I walked in the door at 6:45 exactly.

I looked down the hallway and I could see her behind sticking out from around the corner. "Yum." and I bit at the air. Like I said, I talk to myself a lot.

I took a few steps and turned into the bedroom. I put on civilian cloths and put my gun on my belt behind me under my shirt. I went to the bathroom and washed my hands. Walking to the dinner table I wedged myself in, nice and tight.

My back was to the brick wall right next to the fridge. I always tried to sit facing the door, to protect my wife and family if there was ever an intruder. There has never been one; it was just a little precaution I liked to do.

By the time I situated myself she had a beer sitting at the table and a plate of hot steaming food. It was an Italian dish with Alfredo. I love Alfredo.

I took my first bite and heaven was dancing in my mouth. She was such a good cook, and she made due with the small annoying kitchen and made amazing dishes. She found new recipes all the time and tried to make something new as often as possible.

"So... how is it?" She said exasperatingly.

"Heavenly." I could barely make out the words it was so good.

"Good! How was work, baby?" She always had a little pet name for me. Baby, honey, cutie, she even called me cookie a few times.

"It was good, I made something for you."

"Oh yeah what is it?"

I reached into my pocket and pulled out the key lo-jack and handed it to her. She looked at me confused and she slowly made a smile appear.

"I know it is something amazing, but-." Her face was as if she was trying to figure it out. All it was was a small metal box. There was no way she could know. "What is it?"

"It is a key lo-jack, you go to WWW.PincLo-Jack.com and type in your serial number it is our anniversary and '001' then ta-da! There are your keys."

She smiled and put it on her key ring, and leaned in and said, "You are so smart why have you not been promoted yet."

"Oh that reminds me."

Her face lit up like a Christmas tree.

"Not yet, but I was told, that as soon as there is an opening I would get it."

She spoke with enthusiasm and joy, "That is great, honey! I am so proud of you. I knew you would get noticed sooner or later."

She always was so proud of me. Even this news that was so mundane. She always supported me and made me feel like I was someone important.

"Oh, tomorrow, I would like to stop by and see my dad before we go to the mall." I said and she nodded with no hesitation. Then I asked, "How was your day?"

"Do not even get me started! Well-"

Chapter 3

After dinner and a movie like we do almost every night, we headed to bed.

I say we were going to bed, because I think it is going to be another sleepless night.

After about twenty minutes I can hear her breathing change and I know she is fast asleep. I am staring at the ceiling and making shapes and diagrams like I do every night. I just can not seem to get to sleep. It really is a pain. I want to sleep. I feel like I have to. I just don't do it.

I have seen a specialist, Dr. Coller. He gave me some pills but told me they might be habit forming. No, thank you. That is when I found out about my mental disease.

Low latent inhibition is a problem with your brain. It is more of a personality trait than a disease.

I said that I see things differently, this is what I mean.

When people see a lamp, they possess the image of a lamp, nothing more. I, however, see everything. I see the bulb, the filament in the bulb. I see the screws and the base, the wiring, how it works and everything.

Most people block out that extraneous information; "Stimuli," as my doctor called it. They do that to try not going nuts looking at everything... literally everything. But I have been like that as long as I can remember, so it is all second nature to me now.

I get up and go to the bathroom after a few minutes; I pee and wash my hands. I climb back into bed. There is not even a little slightest bit of me being tired anymore. I am up and ready to start the day. I turn over and look at my clock. "Damn." it is laughing in my face, 2:47am.

Like many nights, I get dressed again and wake my gun up from his comfortable position in line with my socks. I attach him to my belt and walk out of the bedroom.

I leave a note on the bedroom door, so if Sidney wakes up she won't be worried and wonder where I am. She will still wonder, and worry, but I do my part.

I leave the apartment and walk down the stairs, wiggling the post before I go.

I have to have my good luck.

I open the bottom door and New York is a different animal at night. Each alley is like a monster waiting to grab you. There is a flowing fog coming from some of the sewer grates.

The hot air from within the sewer and the cold crisp night forms a fog.

I know it is kind of annoying to see all that… right?

The fog lifts up and fills my vision with the unknown. I can't see the monsters down the alleys. I breathe in and out slowly, knowing nothing is there. Still, I worry.

I walk to the end of the block and go underground to the subway. It is just natural for me to walk and pay my entry and walk over to the platform. It is almost like I do this all the time. My head falls with sadness after that thought.

I look at my watch, 3:00am I look down the tracks and right on time the train pulls in. I hop on the 'E' train and it takes me to 105th. I take a short walk to my favorite spot.

My gun range. It's not mine, I just go there all the time. I feel at home and the people who own it leave it open twenty-four hours a day.

Officers like me get in and shoot for free. I like that. I don't even have to sign in anymore. They just know me and wave me by.

I go back to the range and put up a sheet with five targets on it. It clips nicely into a little rest and it stands before me at three feet away. A child could shoot it and get all five bulls-eyes.

I turn to my right and push a button to send it away on a zip line. I wait about eight seconds and it is nearly seventy feet away. About the whole station could hit these. I keep holding it and it is at about one hundred and sixty feet away. About half of the station could hit these. I keep holding it and holding it.

The poster sized piece of paper is about two hundred and eighty feet away. Only about ten people at the station could hit these. I pull out my gun look down the barrel and squeeze the trigger just once. I turn back to my right and push the buttons brother, the poster is called to me and it comes running. After about twenty seconds its standing in front of me with the center target's bulls-eye missing.

I smiled and send it back, as far as it can go, five hundred feet away. I can barely see it, but I look down my sights and squeeze off all remaining eight rounds. I wait forever for the page to come back.

I never can sleep and I come here about three hours each time, about four times a week. This was the first time in four years I have ever hit it. I may not have had all bulls-eyes but all eight rounds hit the poster and one did hit a bulls-eye.

"Lucky." A voice calls out from behind me.

With out turning around I say, "Nope, skills my friend." I turn around and a man I have never met before is standing behind me with earmuffs on. I have seen him from time to time, just never said anything. He pulls them off and so do I. We are the only people here, so, it is not like someone else is going to shoot.

I said, "No, not totally luck. I am a pretty good shot. I don't think I could do it again but I can try if you want to see."

He was about my age, and was about my height. There were a lot of similarities between us. He looked like someone I knew from a long time ago, or some distant memory, but I could not put my finger on it. If he was a long lost brother I would not have been surprised. His hair was thick and healthy though. "Lucky duck." I thought to myself.

He smiled and said, "I would like that." He paused and held out a twenty. "Wager?" We both put on the ear protection and I went over and grabbed a new sheet.

I put the new target sheet on the clip and waited till it hit the far wall. I turned to him and nodded, I would not have a problem taking this man's money. I put a new magazine in my gun and aimed as carefully as I could. I pulled the trigger and the echo rang off the stone walls. It was a great feeling to pull the trigger and know not a single person could get hurt.

I shot all nine rounds and waited for it to come back. All nine hit the targets. Not one was in the white. I smiled and said, "You must be my lucky charm." I looked back and the man was gone. On the table in front of me was a twenty dollar bill. Nothing more.

I laughed a little. It looks like he didn't want me to rub it in. I picked up the twenty and put it in my pocket. I decided I had been there long enough and headed back home.

On the train ride home I was pondering who that man was the whole time. I had never met him before and he looked like someone I should know. A name could not come to me no matter how hard I tried.

I got home at 4:18 in the morning and slipped into bed at 4:29. For once my eyes fell and I drifted to sleep.

* * *

The alarm started to buzz and I slapped it angrily for waking me for the first time in more than a year. It shouted at me with its mad tones and the face pounding 7:00.

I got up and took a shower. I turned down the hallway, naked as usual and turned the corner into the bedroom. I saw Sidney lying there half naked and covered in a small amount of the blanket and her bra. It was a white lacy one, I really liked it.

I walked around the bed and squeezed one of her breasts. Not in a sexual way, just to wake her up in a strange manor. I had to have my fun every once and a while too, right?

She woke up and smiled, the room just starting to fill with the morning light. She wrapped her arms around me and pulled me back into bed.

I will spare you the details, but you can imagine what happened after that.

I walked out of the bedroom with a huge smile on my face and dressed for the day. I had my gun attached to my belt as always and it was tucked under my shirt.

A few minutes later Sidney came out to the breakfast table. She asked me to make her some eggs.

"I would love to." I said. I could only make a few dishes and she loved me for it. It made her feel better about herself that she could out cook me. I was not offended or anything. I was just happy to be in the same room as her. I gave her a plate with two pieces of toast and two fried eggs on them. Sunny-side over of course.

After the morning routine the clock struck 10:00 and we headed down the stairs to run our errands.

I opened the door to the outside and held it open for her as she walked past me. She hailed a taxi and we told him where to go.

"Oh, I forgot my purse. Can you run up and grab it?"

"Sure thing, babe." I smiled and told the cab driver to wait for me. I sprinted up the steps and all the stairs. I counted every step to and from the cab. I took out my keys at the top of the steps and unlocked my door. I looked around and could not find her purse anywhere.

"Ah ha!" I pulled out my phone and plugged in her serial number and seconds later. The dot was feet away from me. I looked behind the couch and there it was. She had a tendency to throw her purse on the back of the couch and then, when we sat down for the night, it would fall back. "Oh well, I found it."

I threw my phone in my pocket and grabbed her purse. I locked the door and took a step toward the stairs.

My phone came to life singing at me. Edwin McCain's "I'll Be." It was my and Sidney's song. I pulled out my phone and said I would be on my way. I made it to the first floor before I realized I did not wiggle the rail. "Dang." I actually said it aloud. I looked back up the steps, all the way to the third floor. The railing was looking at me, telling me to go back up and wiggle it. Sidney, waiting in the cab pulled me outside. As I opened the door to the city I saw Sidney sitting half out of the cab staring at me as I walked closer. She stared and loved to watch me walk. I loved everything she did. I hopped into the cab and slammed the door. "Off we go."

I tried very hard to see my father at least once a month. It was so hard to do, with all the work I do and that he is so far out of town. He lived in a huge building just east of NYC and had a ton of people to take care of him. I didn't worry.

An hour later I handed the driver a one hundred dollar bill and told him to keep the change and wait for us and there will be more. He nodded as he put the money onto a huge ball of cash and shoved it back into his pocket. I looked in my wallet as I was stepping out of the taxi and saw the twenty from the man the night before. It still ate at me. I had no idea who that was. But hey, he knew I was a good shot.

I walked up a long driveway to a set of steps. I counted them a long time ago and have them all memorized now. Fourteen steps to the first platform, after that, two strides and then fourteen more to the top. Then four strides and turn to open the door for Sidney.

The smell of bleach and disinfectant filled my nose. Sidney did not like the smell but I loved it. It made me remember him. Everything was so clean.

Twenty five strides got me to the elevator and I rode that to the fifth floor. Turn out of the elevator. The carpets were deep red. I thought it looked a little like blood. Not so cool but someone must have liked it. I don't know why, maybe it was supposed to be soothing or something.

The walls were white and the baseboards were made from white pine. It really was a beautiful building, except the ugly carpet. I stepped out to the fifth floor hallway, after another thirty-six steps down the hallway I turned to my right and looked into the room.

Sidney said, "I am going to wait in the hall. Let me know when you are done."

I nodded, pushed open the door and took four steps to my chair at the foot of the bed. A sound all too familiar to me rang in my head. The steady beep of a pulse monitor.

Dad was lying in a hospital bed connected to a bunch of machines. It was nice in a way; I always knew where he was.

"Hit on any hot nurses lately?" the sound of machines keeping my father alive was his response.

"Wow, I knew you were a stud. Even after mom died, I knew you had it in you."

More steady beeps and the sound of the air pumping in through straws down my father's throat into his lungs to be pulled out seconds later.

A tear filled my vision, my world became blurry. I grabbed his foot and said, "I got an announcement. I was told that as soon as there is an opening I would be promoted."

Dad just laid there listening to every word I said. My voice grew weak and my lip curled. "I am going to be a detective just like you, pop." I paused and waited for him to reply. To tell me that he was proud of me. Anything. There was nothing. "I thought about the BB-gun yesterday. It made me want to come and see you."

More beeping and machines.

"Dad, I'm sorry. I really wish they'd caught the guy who shot you. I pray every day that you come out of this." I paused to prevent my throat from catching. "Doctors say that after ten years it is impossible for you to come out. That only leaves us with a few more months." I could barely see him now; the world was blurry with tears.

The constant steady beeping still rang in my ears. I closed my eyes and felt the tears roll down my face and onto my lap.

I patted him on the foot and said, "I pray you are still here. You're still here, right Dad? Daddy?" One thousandth of an inch to the left or right and his brain would have been totally destroyed. I thank God every day that he was still here. "I love you, Dad."

When dad was shot I was down the street playing with my friends. I was playing baseball and after the game I made the long walk home. I entered the door to find my mom lying on the couch crying holding the phone. I was all covered in dust and dirt as I ran over to her. I still remember because I ran over the new white carpet and got mud and grass stains all over them. My mom never said a word about it, she just told me to change and meet me in the garage. I ran up the stairs and changed.

That moment, I did change. I was seventeen. And for the first time in my life I counted everything. I counted the twelve steps down the stairs. The thirty steps to the garage and the six around the car and into the passenger seat. Things changed for me that day. It was not just my clothes. In that moment, everything was different.

I wiped away a tear and walked out of the room. Sidney was waiting for me and she gave me a big hug. She pulled away and I saw her wipe away a tear of her own.

"So? Happy time? We have pictures to take." I said as I smiled.

She smiled and kissed me. "I love you, honey. You are my every thing. Anything you want, baby."

I counted the steps as I left in reverse order. Counting back the time, here in the hospital. I wished I could count back far enough that my dad would not have been shot in the head.

It never worked.

Chapter 4

After we made it outside the building, Sidney looked at me and said, in her cutest voice, "If you want to go back home we can. If you want we can do this next weekend I understand if you just want to go home and relax."

However tempting the offer to sit and play some video games or tinker with something, I just needed to get my mind off of my dad. He was so helpless. Sidney used to come into the room a few times, but after the first year or so it was too hard for her to see "me suffer." My dad was the one in a coma and I was suffering? I looked at the taxi driver still waiting for us. "Let's just go get the picture and I will let you pick something else out at the mall. I love you and I am so glad you are here with me. But, I can't just sit at home right now."

Part of me just wanted to scream. Yell at Sidney for not coming in. To cry, or punch a wall, or go shooting. But I needed to do something nice and mindless for a change.

"If that is what you want." She grabbed my hand and squeezed it twice. I squeezed it back three times. It was a strange little thing that she and I did. It was a way that we told each other that "I love you" without words. It came in handy at a lot of parties and places I could not hear her talking.

We climbed into the taxi and I told the driver to head to the mall.

Off we went. I looked behind us as we were driving away. The driveway seemed like a river taking us away from the pain that was held in the building. So much pain trapped in one area. "God help them." I said to myself.

"Did you say something?" Sidney asked.

"What? Did I say that allowed?"

"Yeah you said something but I missed it."

"Oh, sorry. Never mind."

"Alright." She really did drop it. Some couples would argue and say that it may have been something about her. But she knew without any doubt that I would never, and that if I needed to keep something to myself she respected that. If I needed to talk, I would... boy, would I ever.

* * *

The mall was huge. The ten double doors in and out of the building were not enough for the flood of people. We came here every once and a while to get pictures and some other miscellaneous things. If we didn't want to go to a huge department store and six other places we came here. Everything in the world could be found in this one building.

It was a habit of mine to look at everything. I said earlier that I saw things differently. I did. I never saw just a door, one that revolved around and people could walk in constantly. I saw the axles and the bearings and the glass and every other moving part that was the door. Even the electronic locks that snapped shut in case of an emergency or at close.

The building could have been open twenty-four hours a day and made money around the clock. However, a building this size would have made staffing crazy. Vendor booths, closed at different times during the day, and the mall doors would close at 10:00pm.

I remember a few years back there was a child trapped in the store. The parents left the building and he was playing in the "Toys" department. He fell asleep on a pile of teddy bears and the security guard didn't see him.

They had to open the whole store after hours to get him out. Oh! What an event. It was all over the paper and in the news. The mall settled out of court for over a million bucks. It was kind of ridiculously large sum of money for forgetting YOUR own child in the store.

We walked into the massive building and every time I was in awe. The building at any given time of the day could easily have one-hundred thousand people running around inside. The main lobby was twenty feet tall and in the center of the mall was a huge hole that leads to the roof. Glass panels provided a beautiful natural light that could be seen all the way to the bottom.

I loved to stand in the middle of the opening and look up at the different levels. The hole was twenty eight stories, minus the thirteenth floor... for superstition, I guess. People on the fourteenth floor really knew what floor they were on.

Each level was painted white and reflected all the light further down. The railing was tall, about four feet. A person would have to jump or get pushed off to fall down. Not really something I like to think about anymore.

Last year I was here to keep people at bay from seeing the body of a jumper... there was blood and... well, I will leave it at that.

He jumped from the twenty-eighth floor. That is more than two hundred and eighty feet.

24

He didn't make it.

Being an officer changes you. You see things differently and remember the most horrific events. I had to go to therapy for that. It was my first mangled body. Oops! I wasn't supposed to say that.

We rode the elevator up to the top floor. It was a tradition of ours to walk all the way down. It was about three to three and a half miles to the bottom. We had to stop and get our pictures but that wasn't for a few floors.

The top was a pretty sight. I always went to the edge and leaned way out. Sidney always grabbed me like I was about to jump or something. A huge smile crossed my face as I turned and said, "You just saved my life."

She punched my arm. It was so sweet, her little love taps.

"I would never jump. I could never be without you."

"You know, if you die... I'll kill you. You can't leave me."

We both laughed at the saying we said so often.

I did worry about it. My father went to work like any other day and he never came home. We got word that he was shot and was rushed to the hospital. It was the worst day of my life. Well, maybe my second worst. My worst day... I will have to tell you later.

* * *

After a few floors we realized we passed the photographer. We smiled at each other and turned around and headed back up the steps.

We got to the photo place and the wait was quick, only about fifteen minutes. We decided to go get a soft pretzel while we waited. She was so cute when she ate. It was like she was trying to say, "I am innocent and cute." I could watch her eat all day.

I pretty much inhaled my pretzel and she barely finished hers by the time it was our turn.

We sat down on this wooden box and our bodies faced each other but we looked to the camera. I never liked getting my picture taken. I always felt so ugly. My wife was so pretty but she thought the same way.

She wasn't balding and she didn't have pudgy cheeks. I wasn't fat or anything, just a genetic feature that really made me mad sometimes.

The picture came out great anyway, regardless of the ugly man in the photo. It was against a backdrop of a winter country side or something. It was strange, I didn't realize what drop they used till it was done and paid for. Yeah two people sit on a wooden box in t-shirts in the snow and pose for a camera... right.

However ridiculous, it was a new picture of my beautiful wife. I knew it would look great on my desk at the station.

After a few more floors of walking down and down I heard a phone ringing. It sounded like an old phone. I looked over across the divide and a pay phone was ringing. Odd, I didn't think they could receive calls? Guess they can.

I watched as a man walked over to it and picked it up. He looked at the receiver and hung it back up.

Up ahead was another pay phone. It rang and again a man picked it up and looked at the phone and hung it up.

We walked for a few more floors and the phones, just out of reach were ringing and being answered by people. Meanwhile Sidney was telling me a story that I nodded to even though I wasn't listening. She hated that.

She tested me sometimes to see if I was listening.

"My head fell off the other day. Luckily aliens put it back on with superglue."

I turned and shook my head. "What? Superglue... I am sorry my mind was elsewhere."

"I figured." She said in a deep, upset voice. Then as perky as ever, "Oh sweet, bath lotions! I'll be right back."

"Alright I'll wait out here." Eww!

I hated those stores. I loved how they made her smell but all the smells all at once gave me a headache. I never went into the store, for fear of my brain exploding from sensory overload. I sat down on a bench and waited.

I nearly jumped out of my skin when the phone right next to me rang. I looked around and people walked by without even so much as looking up at it.

I stood and walked the two steps to it. It was a glass booth, not completely enclosed just on one side. It, I guess, gave the illusion of some kind of privacy. The glass faced the divide and on the other side was a few more pay phones lining the railing. There were two phones on each side of me. I stood in the middle as it continued to ring.

I half expected to pick it up and hang up like all the others I saw. Maybe they were just checking the lines.

I picked up the phone and heard static. "Hello?" I could hear myself on the other side like an echo.

I went to hang up the phone and I heard someone on the other end. I couldn't make out what they said.

"Hello?" I asked again. I expected to hear, "Hang up please we are testing the lines." I wasn't so lucky.

"Hello Jayson." The voice came.

My heart skipped a beat. The voice was covered by a synthesizer and it sounded deep and partly robotic. I could barely move.

"I know you are there, Jayson. Now don't hang up or you'll regret it."

"What is that supposed to mean?" I asked trying to cover the fear in my voice.

"Look down, below the phone and behind the phonebook."

I bent down slowly and moved the book out of my way. My heart stopped then tried to catch up with itself. It raced and pounded trying to escape and flee for its life. A large silicon chip with wires and a battery sat below the phone.

The voice said, "I know, I know, I had to put one in every phone to make sure I caught you. And yes it is what you think it is."

My voice was small and weak, "A bomb."

"Very good! This is just a small one, its big brother is somewhere else in the mall."

"Why are you telling me this?"

"Because. I want to play a little game. Do you want to play?"

"No. Not really." I was trying to analyze what was going on. He was in sight of me, that I knew. He could see me and knew every motion I took.

"Well I want you to play so this is how it goes. We are going to be friends you and me. When I ask you to jump, you say..."

"How high?" The words were acid in my mouth.

"Good!" His deep synthetic voice got excited. "I am the puppeteer, you are my puppet. I will control you and you will do what I say or bad things will happen to you. Understand?"

"Yes." I could barely speak. I wanted to scream and yell for help. Who could help me?

"First each bomb is on a timer. The timer is not like any other. It will not go off unless the person is on the phone for more than ten minutes. When they hang up...BOOM!" he yelled it into the phone and it echoed in my head for what felt like hours.

"Alright, what do you want me to do?"

"Below you, the bomb... I need you to disable it. I don't need my puppet to die. Not yet anyway."

The words felt like daggers. "How do I do that?"

"In the top speaker of the phone. There is a magnet to make the phone work. Take the magnet and put it on the steel disk on the bomb. The bomb will activate a switch and the explosive will fall out and land safely on the floor."

"That will break the phone... How will you talk to me?" I still to this day do not know why I asked that.

"Don't you worry your little head. Now go!" The line went dead.

I took out my knife and pried off the speaker cover. Pulled out the small silver looking disk and put the magnet onto a small steel plate. Just as he said, a small putty looking brown slab fell to the ground. My heart raced and I looked at it. I have never seen C4 before. Besides in the movies and it did look just like it. I picked it up. It was really heavy for putty.

My phone chirped and again I nearly jumped out of my skin. I put the phone to my head and said, "Hello?"

"Guess who?" The deep robotic voice said. It laughed and I could barely hold back the tears.

"Alright I did what you asked. What do you want?"

"This is where it starts getting fun." He paused and waited for a response, I didn't give him the satisfaction. "Look down the divide. Two floors down. There is a man on the phone and he just crossed the ten minute mark. Oh no! What is going to happen to him?" He sounded horribly sarcastic. The pain flowing through my mind made my head hurt... maybe, I should have just gone into the smelly store.

"I see him." He was tall and had dark brown hair. He had a nice suit on and had a brief case sitting next to him on the floor. "What do you want me to do?"

"I can disable it from here... but." He paused for a few seconds. "I don't want to I want to see a bang." He laughed again.

Boy did my head hurt.

"There is only one way to stop him. I know you can figure it out and stop him in time." On the other side, there was a pause for a few seconds. "Oh goody! He just said 'goodbye angel' to his little girl. I wonder if that will be her last memory of her father." The line went dead.

I could not think of anything. What am I going to do? It felt like time slowed down. I could yell, but who listens to anyone in New York. Thoughts came to me in a flood.

"Throw something at him. That wouldn't work. You would not be able to hit him. And if you missed he wouldn't even notice it." I said all this aloud talking to myself.

There is only one thing for me to do. I pulled out my gun and aimed it at the man. Kill him and people around him live, or don't and they all die.

That is when a person saw me aiming my gun across the divide. I thought, "Great! Aim quickly."

"Gun!" The man screamed and people came charging at me. I couldn't wait another second. I judged the distance, about four hundred feet.

This was not a good day for me. His hand was heading to hang up the receiver. I squeezed the trigger. It was as if I followed the bullet in slow motion. The bullet left my gun with a plumb of fire and it went screaming for the man. I heard people screaming and running. I heard the sound of the glass in his booth shatter and I saw blood splatter on the floor behind him.

Time continued and I ran for the ledge. I looked down and saw him lying on the ground grabbing at his hand. The phone was swinging on the cord and blood dripped from it.

"Yeah!" I yelled at the coming swarm. They charged at me. I pulled my gun on them and heard my phone ring.

"Get back!" I yelled as I pushed the accept button.

Laughter came from the other end, deep and piercing. "Very good! I meant for you to kill him... but next time I will be much more specific."

"I did what you want now where is it?"

"We are not done yet. And let me say, 'Good Boy,' I didn't want you to give away our little secret about the 'Big Brother'." He paused for a few seconds. "You know, the next one will be so much better. No cops and no talking about me or BOOM!" He took a deep breath and then he started, "Now, this is what I want you to do."

He told me and I nearly lost my pretzel.

Sidney came running out of the stinky room and had a shocked look on her face. "Jay! What did you do?"

I forgot I was still holding my gun and yelling at people to get back.

Think quickly. Faster, faster, FASTER! "Love." acid was building in my throat. "Come here. Will you please?"

Sidney without hesitation came over to me. A robotic voice echoed in my head. "Act well. I will be watching!" I grabbed her and spun her around. I grabbed her neck and held it tight enough to make her face red.

"What are you doing?" She gargled after that, I had to tighten my grip.

I bent down, one hand on Sidney's neck the other on the gun pointing at the group of people. I shifted to my left and grabbed a bag that was sitting inside the last phone booth. I pushed my gunned hand through the strap and flung it onto my back. The bag felt completely empty.

"No one come near me or the girl gets it!" Tears were building. I thought to myself, "Think of something else, not what you are doing... God save us."

I had my back to the railing and slid along it till I got to the bank on the third floor. I walked in using my own wife as a shield. "Put all the money in the tills into the bag. No wrappings and no gimmicks!" I yelled to the tellers. I threw the bag over the counter and aimed my gun at them. I felt like dying. Why did I have to pick that phone up? Why couldn't I just go into the stinky store? Just the thought of it gave me a headache... it could have been all the stuff I was doing. Yeah, that was probably it.

A security guard pulled out a gun and aimed it at me. I turned quickly and aimed mine at him. He was about ten feet away. His hands were shaking. Not a good thing for me. He probably never used his gun and never pointed it at anyone before. There is nothing worse than a man with no experience with guns aiming in a hostage situation. I just hoped that he didn't get scared and pull the trigger and hit Sidney.

I really could not take that chance. "I am sorry." I pulled the trigger and my bullet traveled for his hand. It smacked into his finger and ripped it clean off. He dropped the gun and back away screaming and gripping at his right hand with his left. Blood fell to the floor and one of the tellers threw up all over the ground. Luckily Sidney couldn't see it; if she did she would have done it too. I really didn't need that today.

I walked over to the gun and put it into my pack pocket.

"The money?" I paused as I swallowed my fear. "Now!" I aimed back at the tellers.

My hand was still around Sidney's neck. I squeezed it twice.

I doubt she picked up on that.

She had a look of pure fear on her face. Who wouldn't? I just shot two people in a mall and now I am robbing a bank.

Lord... Please get me and Sidney out of this alive.

Chapter 5

Now that I had the big bag of money that felt like it weighed fifty pounds. I put it on my back and inched out of the bank to the elevators. Sidney was tearing up and crying uncontrollably. The words out of her mouth repeated over and over. "What are you doing?" and "Why?" That was her favorite. Who could blame her? I really hope she understands after this is all done. Why? This is sure to be the worst day of my life. I just know it.

I got to the bank of elevators and thought; this is probably as far as anyone has ever gotten with a heist in this mall without being BLOWN AWAY. "Please don't let that happen to me." I prayed as I waited for the elevators.

The far left door opened and I waited till it closed. I pushed the down button again. I was still waving the gun around and yelling at people trying to get close.

My arm was around Sidney's neck and her face was so red from the crying and lack of air I was forced to give her. If I ever find the puppeteer I will kill him. Mark my words: "I will kill him."

The far right door opened and I backed into it. I pushed the 'close' button and waited till it closed. I turned around and ripped up the carpet in the elevator as it slowly lowered down to the basement. I let go of Sidney and she slapped at my back as I was pulling up the carpet.

"What are you doing? Do you even know what you've done?" she yelled as she constantly slapped my back. I don't think they were love taps.

I didn't know if the puppeteer could hear me so I ignored her.

She continued to hit my back as I pulled up the carpet and found a small key hidden under the padding and dark blue, or gray, cheap carpet.

Like I said before, I saw things much differently than most. I saw a small metal door with a plastic turn lock. It was the kind that could be turned with a quarter. I rotated it with the back end of the key and the door swung open. I could see a key hole under the door and it said, 'Off' and 'Evo'. There were wires I could see under the dark translucent plastic. It was closer to tinted glass. The wires went to another circuit board that connected to the floor selector. I breathed deeply and turned the key to 'Evo' I had no idea what that meant.

The elevator rang loudly and fell below the basement and continued for a few minutes.

The chime rang and the door slowly opened. The floor display red "pst" I didn't want to know what that stood for.

The room was dark and looked like it was not used in months, if not years. One light came on with a loud metallic click and the buzz of electricity filled the room.

Sidney kept hitting me and yelling. All I wanted was her to be safe and us to get out of this alive so I could tell her all about it.

I heard a train whistle and it felt like the loud sound punched me in the face. It was terrible, what was I doing? I was saving lives... I had to keep telling myself that. The bomb could go off at any time. If I do not follow what he said to the letter we could all die.

Sadly, I was his puppet.

A train came to a platform far under ground. The side of the train had a presidential seal on it. "Oh, my God! We are in the presidential underground." It was a huge tunnel system meant for the presidential staff and the president himself. It connected nearly the whole city and had a tunnel all the way to the Pentagon and to the White House. I thought it was just a myth.

A door on the train opened with a rattle of gears and chains, and inside was a big steel box with a lock on it. The lock was un-clicked but hanging on the box.

A pre-recorded message played in a loop. "Put the money in the box. Any hostage you have gets to go for a ride." then it played over and over. The dark robotic voice was like razors in my brain.

"No!" I yelled at the recording. I punched the box and the speaker shorted out. I heard a loud hiss and a gargle.

A mechanical hum came from the train. Above the box on a red LED display was a ticking timer. It said, 4:00 and started to count backwards.

"God help me!" I fell to my knees and prayed as hard as I could.

"What is that?" Sidney asked. Her voice was weak from all the yelling.

"It's your ride." Sadness flooded me. Why did I use her? Why? The question she asked me over and over played in my head.

I was so good at chess. I could out plan and out think anyone. But this guy, this monster, he outsmarted me. He knew I would use her. Damn him!

"No way I am going to get on that thing! What if that box is a bomb?"

I picked up the bag and climbed into the train. It was beautiful. The president may have ridden in this. The box was obviously an addition. I flung open the top of the box and looked inside, it looked empty. I threw the money as hard as I could into it.

I turned back around to Sidney "It looks empty. I never wanted any of this. I am innocent I am telling you the truth!"

I looked at the clock, 3:00 then it sped up to 2:00. I lost a whole minute.

"He can hear us! Get in now. I have said too much already." I lost another thirty seconds.

1:14

"No never. Not without you!"

She still loves me. Even after what I did. I hope she loves me in the morning.

I pulled back my fist and punched her right in between the eyes and she fell limp. I threw her into the train and hit the 'Close Door' button on the inside. I jumped out as the doors were closing. I landed on the platform and turned around to see the clock.

The clock read 0:48 and stopped as the door closed shut. The train started to roll. I walked along side it till it was to fast for me to follow.

It was gone. I had just shot two people, robbed a bank, and gave my wife to a psychopath.

My head pounded and I could not see straight. The world around me got blurry. The ground was unstable.

Right there, on the tracks of the underground train station. I finally lost my pretzel.

* * *

I woke up on the cold stone floor. Puke was covering my t-shirt.

The world was still spinning and dark. I could barely see anything through the fog created in my mind. My head pounded so hard I could barely stand. Each beat of my heart was like rocks being pushed through my brain. It was so difficult to not cry and scream at the horror that just came to me.

The Puppeteers voice rang in my head. I remember every word.

I was at the phone booth in the mall. He told me I had to rob the bank. I needed to have a hostage. The person would have to be a woman and she had to be alive when I got to the end. He told me about the elevator; it had to be the far right one. He told me about the key and that I would be in for a view that few even knew about.

He made it seem like something I wanted to see. Who would care? I wanted my wife!

I nearly threw up again trying to stand. It was a horrible feeling. This was not a dream. It was real and my wife was gone. Taken.

How could I have forgotten? Yes! My first good invention, the key lo-jack!

I pulled out my phone and put in the serial number. It told me she was traveling down through the streets and heading east. It was following a trail I had never seen before.

I put the phone into my pocket and I ran down the tracks after her. I was never going to catch up, but maybe there would be a way to the surface that would get me by all the officers out front.

More than likely they would be people I knew. It is not like I could just slip past them. I had hundreds of eye witnesses that could pick me out of a line up in about one third of a second. Not only that, but they would be reviewing the tapes soon and I would have an APB out on my head. They would have hard proof of what I did.

About five hundred feet down the tunnel there was a hatch about fifty feet above my head with a locking swivel on it. I climbed up the rusty metal latter and grabbed the cold handle. I turned the bar and four locks pulled out of the steel walls. I pushed and the heavy hatch flew open to the outside. The smell of freedom would have been so sweet and bright, but my life was dull now. I had put my sunshine on a train, heading for a mad man, the air smelled like rotten eggs and spoiled milk. Everything was 'shit' to me. I needed my wife back.

I did not realize it before but it was really hot down there. I could feel the sweat pouring down my back and neck. I felt a cool breeze coming from the street. The constant sound of cars rushing by and the din of the crowd filled my ears. I was down a back alley and a homeless man stared back at me like I was from Mars.

I gave him the Vulcan thing from Star Trek and said, "Live long and prosper." I never watched Star Trek but everyone knew that line. I had to do something strange if I wanted to prevent myself from going mad.

He shot back against the wall and shut his eyes and crawled behind a dumpster.

I tore down the alley to the street. People walked past me and looked me up and down with disgust. Then I realized I was covered in my own puke and that kind of pointed me out.

I took off my shirt and threw it into a dumpster. Being shirtless is less conspicuous in the summer than being covered in puke.

My phone chirped and I picked it up as quickly as I could.

"Hello?"

"Jayson what the hell are you doing!" A whispering voice was on the other line.

I should have looked at the caller-ID before I picked it up. It was Vince.

"Vince, I can't talk right now."

"Like hell you can't. I just saw a movie staring you! What is going on? You would never do this. Tell me what is going on."

"No, I wouldn't, and I can't tell you right now! I have to go!" I heard him yell my name as I hung up.

My phone chirped again and I slapped accept without looking again, "Vince I-"

"Vince? Who is Vince... does he want to play too?"

"Puppeteer." The name burned me as it passed my tongue.

"I never would have thought that you would use your own wife as a shield. I just told you to grab A woman." He laughed and it still echoed in my head like an avalanche.

"I wanted someone I know would not try to fight and get the gun away from me or accidentally kill themselves."

"Smart but now she is mine. I like how you play. It makes the game so much more fun."

"Alright you have your money now where is my wife and the bomb?" While I was talking I was keeping an eye on the screen watching my wife's dot fly further and further away every moment.

"There WAS no bomb." His emphasis on "was" made me want to puke again, "There was just the small ones in the phones. Oh and by the way. You are going to get into so much trouble." I could imagine him smiling with his crooked teeth and evil expressions. I honestly had no idea what he looked like. I just can't imagine him looking handsome or something. He could look like a pile of... I have to stop. He continued, "All the small bombs have your fingerprints on them."

"They what?" I yelled and a few people looked back at me. I was walking on the street of New York with out a shirt yelling into my phone. I was just a normal guy. I love this city.

"I have your prints and planted them ALL over the place. Anything that happens will be trailed to you, so I would not go to the police and tell them about us. I want to have some more fun."

"I have had enough of your games. I did all this for you! Now let my wife and I go!" I was standing on a street corner surrounded by about fifty people. No one even looked up. I hate this city.

"There was not a bomb in the mall but oh there is still a few 'big brothers'. And now one is hanging out with your wife. Now I can keep him at bay. However, if you want to let him loose just tell me. You will find little scraps of your wife when I am done." He paused and I held down what ever was left in my stomach.

"How high?" My insides were burning like fire. I could feel every beat of my heart in my head.

"That is my little puppet." I could feel him smirking. "Now, this is what I want you to do-"

I lost it again in the middle of the street.

Chapter 6

After nearly an hour of puking and tying not to kill myself I stood up straight and composed myself.

My watch screamed at me 2:19pm. I walked out of the fast food joint's bathroom and a worker walked up to me and told me I had to have a shirt on to be here. My face got red and I could feel my head throbbing again.

Before I knew what I did my hand ached and the eighteen year old kid with acne all over his face was on the ground holding his nose and crying. People looked up at me and started to walk toward me.

"Oops." I turned around and took off running. About half a block I looked around and no one was following me. My head pounded and my breath smelled like bad mustard and puke. My teeth had a furry feeling to them. I really would have killed for a toothbrush at that moment.

I went to a second hand store and bought a shirt for three bucks. I only had seventeen dollars to my name now. I really hope that I would not need to buy anything else for this... "STUPID GAME!" I grabbed a display at the end of the register and threw it at a window. It bounced off and fell with a loud crash. Random junk flew all over the place.

I thought, "Good keep a low profile Jay. Good job!"

I put on the shirt and walked out of the store without even apologizing for my actions. I looked down at the shirt and it was a rolling stones reunion shirt. I breathed in and out a few times as I walked casually down the street. "Whatever." I said aloud. I was now talking to myself; I am one of those people on the street.

I grabbed my phone from my pocket and looked at the blip. It had finally stopped I nearly hugged a passer-by. I stopped myself to be a little more discrete than usual. I pushed down on the screen, right over the dot. A window popped up and asked me two questions. "Do nothing." and "Save location to clipboard."

I tapped the second and went to contacts. I made a text message to Vince and sent him the coordinates. It was just a long string of numbers but I hope he would be smart enough to figure it out. "I am sure he would be." Stop talking out aloud; you are going to draw attention.

Not ten minutes later I was half way to my second game. - Did I just call it a game? What is happening to me? God save me.

My phone rang and I looked at the caller-ID.

"Vince did you figure it out. Talk to me with no detail."

"Enough about it man! You are so screwed. They already have an agent looking for you. You know what you did right?"

"Yeah I know."

"You know I have to tell someone that I am talking to you right?"

"I know. And you can, just give me a few hours. I know that they won't do anything for the next few anyway. I know they need to have a plan before going after any major... celebrity."

"Just tell me this... Did you have a stunt double?"

"No it was me. Sadly; yes it was me."

Silence. It hurt me to think that he was thinking of me like this.

"Give me like three hours and then scream to high heaven. Alright?"

"Who were you talking to?"

"What!" It hit my off guard. How did he know I was talking to anyone?

"We saw you on a pay phone and on your cell before and after the heist. Who were you talking to Jay?"

"I can't tell you. I have to go." I hung up before I said something to kill my wife.

* * *

Vince put down his phone. He looked over to his left at a man that was tall and had perfect hair and facial features.

The man patted him on the back, "Good work Vince. We will make sure to have you call him and get updates."

"Kiss my ass agent black suit."

"I will let that one go ONLY because you are helping us. But from now on please call me Agent Tanner... thank you."

Agent Tanner turned to the whole station. "What we are dealing with here is a mad man. He has obviously lost his mind and can not control himself anymore."

Vince, being the daring person that he was, stood up and got in "agent black suit's" face. "What makes you so sure? Maybe the man on the other end told him to do it or he would blow the place up. You saw all those small bombs if they all went off at once the whole building could be leveled."

"Yes I did see that. And they all had 'Officer Pinc's' fingerprints on them. He made them. All of them! You even told me that he could make anything, that he was a... hold on I want to get this right." He picked up a piece of paper and read from it. "He is a Brilliant man. A man of above average intelligence and could work for the military someday." He looked up from his sheet. "That is what you said on his last review. Correct?"

"I still don't think he would do it. Maybe the prints were planted. You ever think of that?"

"Well that makes one. Anyone else believe that he is innocent?" He turned and paused for a moment, waiting for anyone else.

Two people raised there hands, then three more. The whole station raised there hands in seconds.

"Told ya! I know my buddy and I know he could not hurt a fly."

"Well I guess I must be mistaken. I know I can't be wrong against all of you."

Vince smiled in victory.

Agent Tanner took a few steps away, "Oh! There is one more thing I forgot to mention."

"What was that? Did you lose a bet? Hmmm?" Vince rubbed his eyes like he was crying.

Agent Tanner sent him a look that could have drawn blood. That shut Vince right up. "No I forgot to mention. The phone call he made, there was no one on the other line." Vince's jaw dropped. "Each time his phone showed ZERO activity. Those pay phones connect directly to security and are recorded in case of bomb threats and other things of that nature. His phone was blank we only heard him talking to himself."

Vince's face grew long and he fell back into his chair. He put his hands on his eyes and could not believe what he just heard.

"So who here believes that our man is still not the guy?" He paused and looked around and saw no one raise there hands. He looked over at Vince. "No words?"

Vince moved his hand like he was going to raise it. Then his eyes grew red and teary. He slapped his desk and papers went flying. He stood and left the room.

"I thought not."

* * *

The world was blurry. Sidney could not remember much from the ride in the train. She did however remember being punched in the face by me. She woke up once in the train for only a moment to be put back to sleep by a gas in the train. Then she woke up here.

She sat in a chair in a room, unknown in size. She looked up and saw the rafters of a basement. She looked around and everything was dark and frightening. Black plastic was draped from the ceiling surrounding her. For all she knew the mad man could be hiding just outside and watching her every move. All the lights were off but she could see a little light coming from the outside over the plastic. The little windows provided little light, but it was enough to see the black plastic prison.

She reached for her face. Her nose felt like it was bleeding or had just been bleeding. Her hands stopped and were held back. Her heart started to race. She looked down and saw rope wrapped around her and tethered her to a chair.

She struggled and struggled but could not move. Her face throbbed with pain and her eyes felt like they were swollen.

"If I get my hands on Jay I will beat the life from him! Does he even know what he is doing?" She could feel her pulse jumping.

The room lit up with a red glow. A large LED display sat tacked to the ceiling. It had a counter on it. It was at "2000"

"Dear God." She struggled and fought against the ropes. She looked at it and saw the counter; read "1946" She struggled a little more and it stopped and froze at "1939"

She didn't move an inch. The display lit up the room with its ominous light.

"The counter is connected to my struggling somehow."

She looked down and saw her chair was on a metal plate, it seemed to be slightly uneven.

She shifted her weight to one side and looked at the counter, "1938"

Then she settled in and tried to make herself conferrable and as still as possible, "1937".

"Oh come on!"

"1933"

Just below the counter was a black bar. It was some kind of display too. It had three green LEDs and then three yellow ones and then three red. The more she spoke the higher the bar would light up.

She thought to herself. *The bar underneath must be a sound detector. All the years with Jay pay off. Unless it he is behind this. Oh I could kill him right now.*

"Hello?" She whispered it. The first LED lit up.

"1932"

She thought, *So, don't speak and don't make any sound.*

She settled in and tried not to panic. *Jay you better not be behind this and you better come as quick as possible.*

"God help me."

"1930"

COME ON!

* * *

I was walking down the street, I was only a half a block away from my next forceful task. My phone rang and I pushed it to my ear, "Hello?"

"It's me. I can't talk for long they may be listening."

"Vince, what are-"

"Shut up and listen. The agent here thinks you did it. I know that is not possible. He is trying to get me to snare you. You have to be safe and figure this out.

"I will! I just need you to get to that spot I sent you."

"I will." There was a long pause. "Jay?"

"Yeah?"

"Are you okay? Like have you been hearing anything when people are not around or seeing things that can't be there?"

"What are you talking about?" I heard a sigh come from the other side.

"Agent Tanner says that you weren't talking to anyone on the phone."

"What? That is not possible. I heard him. He was using a voice changer and his voice will be burned into my memory forever."

"He said they have the recording and it is just you on the phone. There is no one else."

"You have to believe me! It wasn't me! I was forced to do this." The line went dead.

"Hello? Vince!" Nothing.

"I heard that!" The deep robotic voice came through the speaker. My head instantly started to hurt again.

"Look I am sorry! Please don't do anything drastic."

"Drastic like what? Hmmm? Am I insane, am I mad? Drastic like what? This!" the phone went dead and my heart stopped.

The sound did not hit me right away but oh did I feel it. My legs felt like rubber and the ground could not support my weight any longer. I felt the ground slam into my head and the sky was in front of me. Then the sound struck me like lightning.

The street next to me erupted like a volcano and cars flew like tinker-toys. The thick street flew up and concrete flew into the sky and fell like confetti that weighed hundreds of pounds each. A car tire flew past my face just inches above my head and hit a glass window of the shop next to me. Glass fell onto my face and neck; I could feel the little cuts and blood trickling down my open skin. I could not move. Shock had taken over.

I could hear screaming and people coughing and dying all around me. A woman who looked strangely familiar passed over me, nearly stepping on my face, I saw her turn around. She came over to me and looked closely; she looked down and saw me lying on the ground. Her face was covered in dust.

Everything went blurry and silent. I watched as I was dragged by my shoulders away from fire burning in the street and debris everywhere. I saw a human leg coming from under a car. A leash to a small dog was pinned under the car too. The dog sat and looked at his master crushed by the flying vehicle.

No sound entered my ears, just constant ringing. A subway train was sticking out of the street. The nose of the train was pealed back like a banana and fire and residue smoldered licking the sky. Black smoke rolled and filled the air with the toxic smell. A little girl's backpack was lying in the street and she was standing not five feet away from it looking down into the hole. I could not hear her cries but I could read her lips. "Mommy!" she screamed as tears and drool dripped from her face.

All went black.

Chapter 7

I woke and looked at the clock 6:02pm. I had passed out for more than three hours. The room was a place I had never seen before. I heard a voice, far and faint. The sun was up but getting ready to start its decent behind the horizon. The sky was still bright as ever but the faintest hue of orange could be seen coming in through the windows.

"He is awake I have to go."

The world was still blurry and my head throbbed. I could barely hear myself say it but I asked for some pain killers and some water.

A short woman, about five foot and one hundred pounds came back to me and handed me a glass of water and three small pills. I put them in my mouth and bit down on them. I ground them into dust. The taste was like someone dried up piss and made me chew it. I swallowed the water and the taste went with it. I hated doing that but it worked so much faster that way.

"You alright?" The voice was so distant but I could tell the woman was yelling.

"Yeah I am fine. My head is killing me though."

"You have quite the bump and you were bleeding pretty badly. I fixed you up though." The voice was muffled and sounded like she was speaking though a wall.

"I could go for some coffee. I need to stay awake."

I could hear her laugh and say, "It won't be the restaurants." I heard it clear as day. My hearing was coming back.

I looked up and squinted my eyes. "Dina?" I was surprised to see her. "What are you doing here?"

She laughed again. She had a cute laugh it was soft and innocent. I wondered if Sidney found out that I was here if she would beat me up. I chuckled to myself and she said, "I live here silly. I work just down the street." She went into the next room and I could not help it but look at how her body moved when she walked. I took my hand and slapped my face. *You only are thinking that because she saved you and patched you up. Get over it. You have a wife.*

"Nice shirt."

I looked down and forgot I had a rolling stones shirt on. "You like them?"

"Yeah they are my favorite band. What about you?"

"They suck. They're old and should have stayed retired in the seventies." Am I flirting? I don't think so but she is laughing at everything I say. "I have to go." I put my hands on the couch and pushed up to get going.

She tapped my hands and said, "No you don't mister. You are in no shape to move. You need to rest for a while and get your strength." Seconds later I heard her apartment buzzer echo though the house. "Now don't you move I have a friend coming over to make sure everything is alright."

I watched as she went over to the buzzer in the next room and let whoever in. My heart was pounding and my head throbbed. I patted my pocket and my phone was missing.

Dina came back and she had a smile on her face. "Are you feeling better? You are standing all by yourself."

I walked over to her and grabbed her shoulders gently. I looked at her as soft and innocently as I could. "Where is my phone?"

She said, "Umm." It felt like she was stalling to me.

Before she could make up anything I laid a wet kiss on her lips and I could feel the tension on her. I smiled and she pointed to the kitchen.

"It is on the table."

I spun her around and threw my arm around her neck, I flexed as hard as I could and choked her till she passed out. I grabbed my phone and sprinted five steps to the front window. I jumped and smashed through it and bolted as fast as my legs could carry me up the fire escape.

I heard a door bust open in the living room just below me. "N-Y-P-D!" I could hear them swarming around the apartment like ants.

"That bitch sold me out. No tips for her ever again." *But I like that jam... dang it. I'll figure it out later.*

I ran as fast as I could to the roof. I heard someone shout from the window. "He is going up the fire escape get him!" Then I heard a shot. It made my heart skip a beat.

"Stop firing at me I am innocent!" They are firing at me! Why? I didn't do anything. Alright maybe I shot two people, robbed a bank, pissed off a psycho and made him blow up a street, and then chocked a waitress but I am innocent... "I am so screwed!"

I ran along the building and jumped to a neighboring roof. It was only about five feet. I kept running and I could hear at least five fully armed men following behind me. The agent was more than likely just behind them.

I turned around and aimed my gun at them. They were about two hundred feet way. I pictured the targets at the gun range in my mind.

I squeezed the trigger and saw the men fall down right were they stood. "Leg. Leg. Miss. Leg. Leg." Four out of five is not bad.

I kept running and made it to the edge of the building and looked. It was about fifteen feet wide and ten feet down to the next roof. This would be a hell of a jump. I know I could do it but it was high and not something I liked to do.

I took about ten steps back and made a run for it. I put my foot firmly on the ledge and pushed off with all my power.

I could hear the wind in my ear and my feet felt like they were pushing off an invisible walkway. I started to fall and my rolling stones t-shirt flew up and covered my vision. I felt myself falling. Farther than I thought. "Oh my God!"

Then I hit the roof. I landed and rolled onto my back and came to my feet. I jumped in the air and yelled, "Hell yeah!"

I took off running and heard a swat member behind me. I looked back and saw him getting ready for the jump. He looked down at his feet and took a few steps back.

"I could do it; I am not wearing eighty pounds of tactical gear." I took off toward him trying to get his attention before he made the biggest mistake of his life. Correction, it would be the last mistake of his life.

I saw him start running and jump into the air. I charged for him with everything left. I knew he wouldn't make it. I dove and grabbed his hand as he fell past the ledge. He started screaming and I saw his gun fall to the ground below him. I had his left hand in my hands and I squeezed with all I had to keep him from falling.

His right hand was flailing about trying to steady himself. He was dangling off the building like a worm on a hook and I was doing all I could to save his life.

He reached for his pistol with his right hand and aimed it at me.

"Are you an idiot? You shoot me, we both die. Drop the gun and give me your hand."

He looked at his gun and then at me, like he was trying to piece a huge puzzle together with his eyes closed.

"Listen to me dumb ass. Drop the gun or I drop you."

He finally listened and I heard his gun hit the ground below. He reached with his right hand and I grabbed it.

I pulled him up and he fell to the roof. I landed next to him and I could not stop panting.

"I'm sorry about this." He looked over at me and I elbowed him in the face. He screamed and grabbed at his nose. I did it again and he screamed louder. One more time and the screams stopped and he fell limp.

I got up and looked along the roof line. Just over three hundred feet away I saw Agent Tanner looking at me like a prized trophy to a hunter. His dark blue jacket read "F.B.I." It really was a scary thought, to have an agent hunting you like a deer.

I flipped him off and took off running the other direction. I was not going to wait to see if he made it over the gap or not. This battle was mine; however, there was still more battles to wage.

I looked down at my watch. 6:29pm. "I only have an hour and thirty-one minutes to complete the task or something bad is going to happen."

I looked at my phone and my screen was cracked. It was dark, but a scattered image came on. I could not use it anymore to track my wife. I had no way to get any kind of detail. I pushed send; send and the phone came to life. "At least he can still reach me."

* * *

Vince was well out of the city now. He looked at his map and this was where he needed to be. The coordinates led him to this, an abandoned warehouse just out of the city. There was not a single soul for miles.

Vince got out of his squad car and walked over to the steel door to the warehouse and turned the handle.

It was locked. He shook it, as if that would unlock it. It was a habit, who doesn't do that?

He saw there was an open window to the left on the second floor. It was broken and all the glass was missing.

He looked around for anything he could use to get inside and he could not find anything. He grabbed his phone and flipped though his contacts to 'Pinky' He hit send and waited.

"Hello?"

"Jay it's me, Vince."

"Vince what's up? Are you at the location?"

"Yeah I am. But I can't get in. It is some kind of old warehouse. There is a second story window but it has to be at least twenty feet up and nothing I can use for a rope or anything. What do I do?"

"Did you check the front door?"

"Yes, do you think I am some kind of idiot?"

"Is the door steel or wood?"

"Steel. Why?"

"Does it have a pull handle or a rotating lock?"

"Hold on." Vince walked over to the door and then came back, "It looks like it is just a pull handle."

I was thinking for a few moments, trying to imagine every possible plan. "Dang that would be a bad idea. We can call that plan B." There was another long pause and then, "Okay. Did you bring your car or the squad car?"

"The squad car. Why?"

"Okay listen..." there was a bunch of wind in the background and Vince could barely hear me.

"Jay! I can barely hear you! Are you running or something?"

"No time just listen." Wind was rushing past the mike and caused a bunch of static. I was so out of breath I am surprised he could understand me at all. "Grab the tire iron from the trunk, the bent angle one. Then go under the hood of the car. There should be a huge length of wire running through the engine to the lo-jack system. Cut out the wire and tie it around the iron and throw the iron through the window. Use the wire as a rope and crawl through. Call me back if that doesn't work so I can give you plan B."

The line went dead.

Vince ran to the trunk and popped it open. He rummaged through the stuff till he got the iron. He held it firmly in his hand and said, I hope I know what you are talking about Jay. He ran around to the front driver door and opened it. He popped the hood and took a deep breath.

Was he ready to destroy a section of his car? Would there be more than twenty feet? Vince got to the front of the car and lifted up the hood. He put the locking stick into place and looked around.

"I don't know anything about cars. What wires?" Vince looked around and saw a NYPD symbol on a black box, there was a long set of wires coming out of it. There was a red, green, black, orange, and a yellow wire all traveling to different parts of the car. He could not help himself. "Wow that is a lot of wire! How does he know all this stuff?"

He grabbed the base, where they all met the black box and yanked as hard as he could. He pulled out and ripped the wire. It was only about fifteen feet long. A lot of profanity left his mouth as he reached for his phone.

"Hello? Vince?"

"Yeah it's me. I ripped the wire. It isn't long enough. What do I do?"

I paused for a long time, I was tracing over every schematic I could think of. "You're not going to like this, plan B." I told Vince what to do and hung up.

Vince swallowed and said aloud to himself, "Alright I hope this works."

He wrapped the wire around the iron as many times as he could. He connected each length to each other and left only the red and the black unwrapped around the iron. Then he connected the tale end of the red wire to the positive node of the battery and the black end to the negative node of the alternator.

The words rang in his head. "You may kill your car."

"If this doesn't work I am going to blame this all on him. I am not going to buy another squad car."

Vince put the wrap of wire and tire iron in through the door handle. He got back into his car and maneuvered his car to have the front facing the door.

He turned the ignition and the iron slammed against the door with tremendous force. He kept the car idling and ran to the iron. He pulled with all his might and the iron slid an inch away from the handle. He could here the other side of the door squealing like an injured animal. He pulled and pulled with everything he had and the bar moved an inch more. Then he turned around and put his foot on the tire iron and pushed with his legs. The iron pushed a foot to the middle of the door.

Vince was sweaty and his arms were sore. He put his hand on the handle and pulled. The door came open. He looked at the other side of the door and the metal lock was pulled to the center of the door.

"Jay you are one smart guy! You made an electromagnet to switch the inside lock to 'un-lock'! Brilliant!"

Vince ran back to his car and turned it off. He didn't want the battery to blow up. He reached over and grabbed the cars shotgun and a flashlight from the front seat. He took a long deep breath and ran into the dark building.

He looked into the empty void that was the warehouse. Above him were pulleys and tracks all along the ceiling. Wire hung from everywhere. In the far corner was an office on the second floor, the windows were broken and graffiti was all over the place.

In the middle was one dim light, it was on and glowing the center of the room. It flicked off. Vince jumped out of his skin and turned to find the switch. He was shaking, he had done practices in the academy but nothing trained him for this. The light flicked back on and then off, then back on again. He nearly pissed himself from fear, but thought it was just a dying bulb. "Please be just a dying bulb." He said aloud.

He walked carefully to the center, under the light. He was out in the open; anyone could peg him off with no problem. Below the light was nothing but dust. He aimed his flashlight at the ground and saw markings like this was some kind of manufacturing plant or packaging place. There in the dust was the small metal box, the key lo-jack.

Written in the dust was a note. "You just lost a string." It was signed, "- Puppeteer."

* * *

My phone rang and my whole body shook. "Hello?"

"I said to not come after me. I said no cops and you could not listen could you?"

"But I-"

"That is enough! There are penalties to cheating in my game." His voice was angry, violent even. The synthesizer cut out at one half of a second and I got a glimpse at his voice. It was sounded healthy. The man was, more than likely, in his early thirties maybe his late twenties, definitely male.

I could barely concentrate on what he was saying I tried so hard to engrave that sound into my memory.

"Did you hear me?" It sounded more like a demand than a real question.

"I am sorry, my phone cut out."

"No it didn't. Now, pay attention. This is the result of your cheating. Take your gun. Put it to your left forearm in between your elbow and wrist and pull the trigger." A pause, "OH! And make sure the safety is off and it's loaded. I do not want you to catch me again." Click.

I looked around and saw a large group of people around. This probably wouldn't be a good place to do it. I turned down the next street and wondered into a back alley and hid behind a dumpster. I didn't want to draw any more attention to myself.

I pulled out my gun and checked the magazine for rounds. There was a few left. I took off my belt and bent it into three segments and put the bunch of leather into my mouth. If I had to shoot myself I didn't want to bite off my tongue too. I put the gun against my forearm and bit down, hard on my belt. I don't think I had ever been that nervous and I squeezed the trigger.

SNAP!

"Damn it!" I turned the gun around and flicked the safety off. I put it back to my arm and got ready again. Both of my hands were shaking and my heart rate spiked. I breathed in and out rapidly and started to squeeze the trigger.

BLAM! Screaming echoed off the walls of the alley and blood shot from my arm. I fell over and could barely move.

Seconds later my phone chirped.

"I did it."

"I know. Good job my little puppet. Now that you have lost a string you have an extension to your task. You have till 8:15 to get it done. Or Boom!" There was a quick pause, "Understand?"

"Yeah, I got it." I looked at my watch. 7:01.

"God help me... please."

Chapter 8

I started my run down the street. I didn't care about appearance anymore. Let people think what they want I need to get to the next task before 8:15 or something big is going to blow.

I was dripping blood down my arm. I tied it off with a section of my jeans. I cut the bottoms off about five inches thick. I used one as a wrap and the other to hold it into place. The denim in my jeans would hold in my blood a lot better than my crappy rolling stones t-shirt. Besides, I don't even want them touching my blood.

I reached the location of my task at 7:43pm. I still had a little bit of time but I was really out of breath. There would be no way I could do it like this. I needed to calm down.

I looked around for anything that would or could put my mind at ease. Across the street was a liqueur store. "That will do."

I looked both ways before crossing the street and I walked in and checked my wallet. I didn't have any cash. "What happened to my seventeen bucks?" I said aloud. I had trouble standing, my heart was racing. "That bit-" I cut myself off. Dina must have taken it. Now after this is all done, I will not go back there.

Alright I still will. Is it my fault I have an unhealthy obsession with that jam?

I looked back down at my wallet sitting empty in my hands. I still had my credit card but I was sure they would track it here before I needed to finish.

I walked around the store to the far back and picked up a bottle of Vodka. I held it above the aisle and yelled, "How much is this?" to the clerk. As he was looking at the fifth in my hand I put a pint into my back pocket. My left arm was burning as I gripped the little plastic bottle and put it into my pants.

He looked it up and down and yelled, "Nineteen bucks."

"Dang!" I put it back on the shelf and walked out without him even noticing me. Or the trail of blood I left.

I crossed the street and into the back alley. I ripped the screw top off and threw it on the ground. I put the bottle to my mouth and poured it in. It burned like fire but I could barely feel it over the fire burning in my heart for Sidney. The picture of us was still in my mind. Maybe after this is all done, we will go out to a snowy country side and wear t-shirts, getting our picture taken. But who was I kidding? She was still missing.

The bottle was empty faster than I thought. Anger boiled over in my head, I could not take it anymore. I was out of vodka; it did nothing to stop the feeling of my heart being ripped out. I needed to calm down, I told myself to breath. Why can't I breathe?

"AHHHHHH!"

I tried, oh how I tried to keep my cool. But there is a limit to everyone and I could not take it anymore. I squeezed the bottle in my hands and threw it against the far wall. It shattered into countless pieces. The glass looking back at me in misery from the violence I just inflicted on it.

I could not hold in my emotions anymore. I fell flat on my face and held my head as I cried loudly in the alley. I wailed and tears poured from my face. I thought about Sidney. She must have been so scared. I pounded my right fist to the ground and then I brought up my left arm and screamed in pain.

The booze did nothing. I still was aware of everything and I had to go through with it. Or my wife might die.

I stood up and walked further down the alley. I looked behind a dumpster and there it was, just as he told me. It looked back at me with anticipation, a wooden crate.

"Damn it." I said as I sighed. I was hoping it would not be here.

I lifted the top and it was empty.

"No! No... no... no... NNNOOOOO!" I lifted the box and threw it clear across the alley completely ignoring the pain in my arm. I searched through the dumpster, there was nothing.

"Where is the shotgun? What am I going to do now?" I yelled and screamed; the echoes bounced off the walls and rang clearly in my head.

I picked up my phone and looked through my received calls. The phone was scared and broken, just like me. Even though it has been through hell, it still was trying to help. The phone was hard to read but I could see the contacts, barely, but I could.

I had to talk with the puppeteer. He had to have a back up plan. He could not assume everything would go the way he wanted; people in New York stole everything. I flicked through the list of calls. My heart sank lower than hell itself, I could not find the puppeteers number.

I looked and looked. There were no calls coming in other than Vince. Not a single one. The last one from anyone was two days ago from Sidney.

Was this all in my head? Could it be?

"Am I the puppeteer? Am I really going mad? NO! It can't be."

"Why not?"

I turned and drew my gun. My left arm was on fire but I steadied myself and aimed for his head. It was the strange man from the gun range. I got a good look at him again. He was about my age, my height, and my build.

Oh my God I AM going insane.

"You may want to lower your gun. You don't want to kill me now do you?"

"Why wouldn't I?"

"You have not been sleeping for what? For more than a year now? You have created someone to talk to in your night awake in the gun range. This is not the first time you have found out about me?"

"It isn't?"

"No. We have had our little spats your whole life at least for ten years or so."

"So why do I not want to kill you?"

"You would kill yourself. Shooting me is shooting you. You do not want to do that. That is why all the bombs, all the random equipment, they will find will have your fingerprints on it. We have the same prints because you and I are the same person."

That can not be true.

"Why can't it be true? I just read your mind. I am in there with you. I know everything about you."

"So why punish myself? Why do this?" I asked, nearly pleading with myself... I guess.

"It is just that. A punishment, you are torturing yourself for what you did."

"And what did I do?"

"What do you remember about the day you father was shot?"

Cold sweat dripped down my back. "I remember everything. I remember playing ball with my friends down the street. I remember ruining my mom's carpet with mud. I remember changing; I started to count everything."

"That was not the only thing that changed, you made me up there, that day, that second. I was created and I covered up what happened that day."

"Enough with the run around. What happened?"

"I am so sick of telling you this! But fine." The puppeteer paused and leaned to one leg like he was tired of talking. "You did it. You shot your father."

My heart stopped. Stopped, stopped. My body was dead in that moment I went cold and I swear I saw death. I came to before I even blinked. "I did what?"

"You shot your father. It was your day to sneak out with him. You did it all the time remember. You went to go shooting with him. Why do you think you count everything? You thought the gun was empty. He always told you to never play around. You didn't listen. You pulled the trigger, playing around and there was one bullet left." The puppeteer clapped his hands and yelled, "Blam! Bye-bye, Daddy."

I could not believe it. I could not do that. I do not remember a thing. Don't people in movies remember it once it is told to them? Why can I fully remember the baseball? Not a single memory is coming back. Am I that lost?

"I made a nice cover for you and took away all the pain. I will hold on to it for you forever more. But there is still a pressing matter at hand."

"And what is that?"

"I still have your wife. Well, WE still have your wife. And you don't know where she is because I won't tell you."

The world got dark. My hands started to shake. My head was heavy and my eyes rolled into my head.

"Nightie-night. I'll see you soon."

I passed out and fell to the ground. The puppeteer was right on the nose. If I did not go through with the task there would be another big bomb. My watch read 8:16. I don't think there could have been a bigger bomb than that kind of news.

* * *

56

I woke to the sound of my phone ringing. I looked at the clock. "10:38" Vince was calling me.

The sky was dark and air cold. New York is alive, it never sleeps, and everyone thinks that it slows down at night. It doesn't. The street was a busy as ever and cars and people walked as if it was five o' clock on a Friday. I stumbled to my feet and leaned against the brick wall.

"Erggg! Hello?" I said as I tried to focus.

"Jay it's me. I am standing outside the station. I sent some people to where the location was. It was nothing. Only the key lo-jack and a note."

"What did the note say?" I knew what it said.

"It said, you just lost a string... or something like that. It was signed 'Puppeteer.' That was not the troubling part."

"And what was?" It was in my handwriting? It had my fingerprints were all over it?

"It was in your handwriting and your fingerprints were the only ones we found. Come on man. This is getting harder and harder for me to believe that it wasn't you. Tell me something anything that can prove me wrong."

What could I say; my own phone proved it was me. How could I tell him? *Vince I did it. I am the puppeteer.* Oh how I wanted to say it. "I can't. I don't know anything."

"Well I still believe you. I won't give up I promise. I love you man. I would do anything for you."

"There is one thing you could do for me."

"Name it."

A deep long sigh. "If I am going mad, I should know about some things. Look up and tell me whatever you can find about schizophrenia."

"Skittle what?"

"Multiple Personality Disorder, MPD"

A really long pause. "Sure thing, buddy." Click.

What am I doing? I have my wife locked up somewhere. I needed to find her.

"Think. Think. Think. If I was a mad man, I am a mad man. Where would I put my kidnapped wife?"

Somewhere no one else would look. Somewhere secluded, away from everyone.

"The tracker was heading east for quite some time. The warehouse was out east. I guess I will start there."

I hailed a taxi and told him to drive north-east out of the city. Let me tell you, it is hard to get a taxi during the day. It is a thousand times harder at night on a Saturday. But I digress, I rode along for nearly an hour before I realized I did not have one cent to my name.

"Pull over here."

It was some residential place, homes every which way. This is the kind of place I would like to live, out of the city and the crappy apartment. Something like where I grew up.

"That's it!"

I stepped out of the cab and walked to the driver side window. I was really surprised that he didn't pull out a gun when I even got out of the cab without paying. I guess I have that kind of look. Even in the bloody rolling stones t-shirt and cut up jeans and tourniquet… this is New York.

I had him roll down the window and I pulled out my wallet. It was empty but I needed him to be off guard. I punched him in the face and he went limp. His foot fell off of the break and the car started to creep forward at about two miles an hour.

I looked around and the little community was sleeping. It was 11:57pm. There was no one around, finally a break. I opened the door and pulled him out as the car crept forward. I hopped in and slammed the door shut.

I lurched forward and slammed on the brakes. I threw it into reverse and then I rolled the window down again. I poked my head out and looked at the man on the ground.

"Sorry." He couldn't hear me. But hey, it was mostly for me.

I rolled up my window and drove off. My childhood home was still in my mind, it was less than an hour away.

It was a nice house I had kept it up and running for years, I was hoping to keep it till I wanted it. Sidney and I had thought about moving here but the job in New York was nice and we had a little place of our own. Plus, the commute would be nearly two hours, and now it was only about fifteen minutes.

My mom was the last resident… she passed away in that house. I don't think that she could handle what happened with Dad. She got sick after the news.

I truly think that there is just one person for everyone. Once my dad was shot it was too hard for her to continue. She got sick and doctors really couldn't find out what happened to her. After more than a year she got really sick, and then she couldn't move on her own.

Two years after my dad was shot she passed away. It was a horrible thing for me. My father was in the hospital and my mother was dead. Her insurance paid for most of the doctor bills and I was left with a few thousand to pay for most of the up keep of the house. I could not bear to get rid of it.

Chapter 9

I pulled up to the house and looked at my childhood. The life I lived was great. We were not very rich but we had a home and food on the table every day. Could I complain?

The house was part of a community. It was required that we kept the lawn trimmed and the house painted and clean.

I paid someone once a month to mow and rake leaves in the summer and fall. I had someone come here and paint the house once every three years. My mom couldn't do it the last time so I paid someone and I kept him in my contacts.

I pulled into the driveway and looked up at the home. It was a small house. The majority of the color was a light sky blue. There was white trim along the length and around the windows. It was a nice home and Sidney and I were going to move in but... to many bad memories and it was too far from work.

The lawn, for the most part, was green. It looked like a local dog had gone in the lawn a few times. There were brown spots and piles of... you know what, scattered around.

I walked up to the front door and turned the knob. It was locked.

I usually keep the keys at home. "If I really am the puppeteer, I would have the key on me. Right?" I did not know who I was asking.

I looked in all my pockets, a sigh of relief. I may not be him. That is when my heart stopped again. I felt a sharp metallic object in my shoe.

"Oh no." I could barely look down let alone take off my shoe. I had to know. I pulled off my shoe and held it upright in my hand. I put my left arm out. It burned from the gunshot. Then the real pain started. A little tan key fell out of the shoe and landed in my hand.

"Why? Why? WHY!" Why would I do this? How could I do this?

The key looked back at me as I felt my pocket vibrate and heard it ringing.

"What!"

"Dude sorry. I catch you at a bad time?"

You are kidding me. I paused for some time.

"Oh.. yeah sorry. Well I got you a bunch of info. You still want it?"

"Yeah lay it on me." I pushed the phone in between my ear and shoulder as I put the key in the lock and turned it. It opened.

"Turns out... Skittle... whatever... is a problem most of the time triggered by a horrific event. It says here that most occasions only hear things such as whispering or voices. Rare occasions can be severe enough that the person can have separate lives. Separate jobs and separate everything. Sometimes it can be so different that they can have different handwriting and even speech patterns." He paused like he was reflecting on what he just read. "This is kind of cool. How come I didn't know this?"

"Does it say how to stop it?"

"Yeah hold on." He came back within a few minutes. "Therapy."

"Anything else, anything at all will be helpful? I may need to do something."

"Are you not telling me something Jay? I am talking to Jay right?"

"Shut up man."

"We have to laugh or we... would go insane." He stopped like he was trying not to offend me. That hurt a little.

"No I am telling you everything I know. Anything other than info that is useful?"

"Yeah, even rarer is the case; that the two OR MORE personalities do not get along. They some times result in the death of the individual. They would think they are killing their most hated enemy and they are holding a gun to there own head or something." Another long pause, "This stuff is so cool! I am totally going to get into this some more." He paused and I could hear him flipping though pages. "So where you at Jay?"

"I am at my old... I can't tell you. I wish I could. Goodbye Vince." Click.

* * *

Vince hung up the phone and he looked up at Agent Tanner. "I got all I could. But he still won't tell me."

"My old... What? Where is he?" He slammed his hands down on the desk and pushed his nose right up against Vince's face. "You tell me now. Or I will lock you up for aiding and abetting."

"I honestly don't know. Now get your face out of mine and get your dead rat breath away from me." Vince stood up and walked out. He grabbed his jacket from the coat rack and walked out of the station.

Agent Tanner watched him leave and get into his car. He put his hand over his shoulder and formed it into a cup. An officer put a set of car keys into his hand and he rolled up his jacket sleeves.

"He will lead me right to him." His face formed an ear to ear grin.

* * *

Sidney could hear a door opening above her, and minimal commotion. She looked up at the ceiling and feared the worst. The floor was creaking and making all kinds of noise. She looked at the counter shining like the sun in her face.

"748" Then another step "746"

Her time was coming to and end. She wanted to scream. What if it wasn't help? What if it was the psycho that put her in this mess. She prayed and prayed she had to believe that it was not Jay's plan to have her be like this. She knew he would come for her. She had to believe he would rescue her. He was so smart she knew he would figure out this bomb and all the traps, she knew he would out think and out smart the monster behind all this.

"Hello." She whispered it as quietly as she could. The LED sound register did not even light up. "God save me."

A tickle in her throat made her wince. She had to sneeze badly. It burned in her mouth and then in her nose. She knew she couldn't help it. Think about something else.

"Ahhhhh." Oh please no.

"Ahhhhh." Don't do it. Stop yourself.

"ACHOO!"

The sound display beeped as it flew into the red. It was the first sound it made.

"644."

I lost one hundred for sneezing. What happens if someone finds the bad guy and then they shoot him? A gun shot could push it down to zero. "Jay, please hurry up."

Chapter 10

I pushed open the door to my old house. I looked around and saw so many memories. The BB-gun was hidden in this closet. I opened the door slowly.

I flattened my hand and slapped my face. "Get yourself together. Sidney might be here."

I looked down the hallway and up the steps. Flashes of my childhood past hit me like a ton of bricks. "Sidney!"

I heard screaming. Loud but muffled screaming, coming from the basement. She knows I am here. She hates me. What have I done to her?

I grab the door handle to the basement and I hear a footstep behind me. I whip around and see the puppeteer standing. I see, me... standing there.

"I wouldn't open that if I were you... and I am, so don't."

"And why wouldn't I?"

"There is a bomb and it is set to go off as soon as the door is opened, moved or tampered with." He paused and watched me take my hand off the knob. Slowly, his face lit up and a smirk took over. "That is a good little puppet. I know I don't want to die. So I know you don't ether."

"So what do you want from me? I know you are me and you must want something."

"What I want is not important. I want what you want. And you want to go to jail for what you did. You want to have the blame finally on your own shoulders. You want to have the person responsible for your fathers shooting to face justice. You can do that. Give yourself up. Tell them what happened and have them punish you to the full existent of the law."

"So I want to put myself in jail? I am insane, and it was an accident."

"Your father, yes! That was an accident. However, shooting those people, and robbing the bank. All those assaults, those were all on you." His voice was like poison in my heart. He was absolutely right. I was so screwed and I was going to go to jail for all of it. It was me. I was insane but I knew full well what I was doing.

"Why? Why go through with it. I would get more satisfaction just blowing my head off right here and now."

"So go ahead and do it. Why not? I really don't want to die but hey, if you do I guess I do."

"I could just open the door to the basement... it would be quick." I stood up and walked over to the door and grabbed the handle.

"I still wouldn't."

"Why not? I don't like guns. Now I know why." I shot my father.

"Well if you turn that handle you will kill your wife down there too."

My heart sank. I forgot she was here. I needed someone to disarm this bomb and let her out. But if I call someone I would get arrested and I would not have the time to get my own shot off. "Well this sucks."

"You're telling you. I know."

I could hear the sound of cars hurtling toward my house. I could hear someone yelling from outside.

. I grabbed a pen and wrote "bomb on door to basement." on a piece of paper. I grabbed my gun and put it into my right hand. I put the barrel against my head and cocked back the hammer. I could feel my teeth chattering against the end.

The puppeteer sounded urgent, "They are coming. We only have seconds. Do it!"

I could feel my finger squeezing the trigger. The blast would come in seconds.

I heard a loud crash as the front door was kicked in. I pulled tighter and tighter waiting for the bullet to scream out of the barrel and into my head, ending all this pain.

"BANG!"

The sound was peaceful. The lights in the room got really bright and I saw everything I ever did in my life flash before my eyes. I could feel nothing. There was no pain. The heat of the bullet was still burning in my mouth, I felt the liquid life pouring out of me and the pain hit me all at once.

"Jayson!" the voice was a different world.

I heard footsteps coming over to me. I was on the ground. The cold tile was pushing against my face. Blood squirted out of my head and I could taste the salty flavor.

Then I saw Vince look like he had seen a ghost. He pointed his gun down the hallway across the kitchen. Stood up and took aim.

Blam. Blam. Blam. The sound of gunshots, it was so muffled. He swore a few times. He ran back over to me and said, "Oh my God! What did you just do?" He ripped his shirt off. He was much stronger than he looked. He pushed his shirt against my head and grabbed his radio. The world started to fade.

I heard him screaming into his radio, "Officer down. I repeat Officer down. I need a paramedic at One-Two-Two-Four-Niner Broadview road." he looked down at me and screamed. "Don't you leave me? Jay? No! JAY!"

The world was gone. Darkness was all I saw.

Chapter 11

I woke to the sound of beeping and machines running my life. I opened my eyes and I could feel that something... someone was next to me.

"He is awake! Jayson! Jayson?" I felt my whole body ache and I knew someone was shaking me.

"Stop it. Let me sleep."

I felt a feeling I loved more than my own life. A kiss on my lips. Oh, I knew those lips. "Sidney? You're alive."

"And so are you, you lucky dog."

"What happened?" I went to reach for her and my hand was stopped. I looked down and felt the cold hold of handcuffs. "Shit."

"You shot yourself. The bullet went in through your cheek and tore in and blew your teeth out. No major brain damage. You will have dentures but you're going to live. The handcuffs are well... because of what you did."

"I am so sorry honey. I have gone mad. I am crazy you know."

Sidney paused and looked over her shoulder. "I will let the expert tell you all about that."

Vince came in. He was wearing a suit and tie. He looked weird

"You hate the monkey suits. What are you doing?"

"Well I quit the force. Really this stuff fascinates me so much. But I am here to talk about you."

"Oh no. Are you going to be all 'Shrinky' on me?"

He laughed and said, I have only just started class... so no. But I am going to tell you something that you will like to hear."

"And what is that? They are going to give me the death penalty?"

"No. You are not crazy."

My heart skipped a beat. I know because the machine attached to it told me.

"The person you saw, 'The puppeteer'."

"Yeah?"

"He is now the F.B.I.'s MOST wanted criminal. He tricks people. He is a genius in the highest respect of the word. He alters his voice and patterns of movement a bit like the victim to make them think they are him. Then he sends them around doing horrible things. He tells them they are insane and then most end up killing themselves. Only one person has survived to talk and he didn't make it to the hospital before telling the police exactly what happened. You're the first to live."

"You have to be fu-"

A nurse barged in. "Your heart rate is skyrocketing are you alright?"

I breathed a few times and calmed myself down. "Yes I am fine. Thank you."

Vince continued. "I don't think you will have too much trouble getting out of this. You may have to spend like thirty days or something in minimum security. But that should be about it."

"Vince."

"Yeah Pinky?" I didn't mind it so much coming from him. He did, after all, save my life.

"I need a minute."

"Take all the time you need." He stood up and hugged Sidney. He left the room and shut the door behind him.

Her voice was like an angel. "Why don't you get some rest? I am worried about you. You did shoot yourself."

"I am so sorry for what I did. I will have to tell you all about it someday. I love you so much and I am so sorry I pulled you into all of this."

"Honey... yes I was mad at you. I could have ripped your head off. But I see why you did it. You did all of it for me. You used me because you knew I would not fight back. You did all the horrible things because you thought, and were right, a psycho was after me. I love you and I will never hold a grudge against you."

"He told me some horrible things honey. Things that I was sure I did not do. But they are stuck in my head now and I think I may have done a few of them."

"Like what?"

"He told me that I was the one who shot my father. He told me that I blocked it out."

"He told a lot of people a lot of things. It was all part of his plan to manipulate you into killing yourself. But he was not you and he would not have known."

"There is still some doubt, I fit the profile. A traumatic event can cause M.P.D. and I did. I may have blocked it out. I could have done all those things."

"You loved your father. You still do. I don't think for one second that you would ever do any kind of harm to him. And that is my expert opinion. And I am your wife... so I am always right." She smiled. Oh, how I love her smiled. "Let me ask you this. Did he tell you about your father or did you say it and he picked up on it?"

A smile slowly crept over my face. "He picked up on it... you are so smart. AHHH! I love you."

She stood and kissed me on the forehead. "Now you," She pointed at me like I was going to run somewhere. Ha! "Get some sleep. I mean it!"

She left and came back in the door. "Oh I was meaning to ask you."

"What is that honey?"

"When they found you, you were wearing a rolling stones t-shirt. Do you like them or something?"

"Do you like them?"

"No they suck. They're old and should have stayed retired in the seventies."

"God, I love you."

She smiled and left.

* * *

Ten days later I was finally released. I talked the situation over with Agent Tanner. He told me that the F.B.I would make sure I do not see the inside of a cell if I promised to testify on behalf of the case.

Like I was going to turn that deal down.

* * *

Sidney and I had talked about what had happened.

Apparently she never saw the guy. He had her drugged the whole time and put her into places that she could not see him. She told me about the rescue after they got into the house they sent in bomb squad.

I talked with bomb squad and they told me. They used tiny lasers to burn a hole in the door and stop the bomb. I did not know this but they froze it through the door. They tore a hole in the door with the laser and poured liquid nitrogen down through the hole onto the bomb. The bombs battery froze and it shut off. They took the door off and crept slowly down the steps.

They said there was a black ring of plastic in the corner of the basement. There was wire coming in and out of the tarp. They could hear someone on the other side saying to keep quiet.

They found the bomb. I was told, and kept it from Sidney, that is was big enough to level the building and all the houses around it. They found the different triggers and disarmed it from the base of the bomb.

Sidney was crying so much when they got her out of the chair. I was being escorted out to the hospital but they said the counter was at "14."

Sidney was a sneeze away from dying. I was never so happy to see her alive and well.

* * *

Vince told me that he saw the "Puppeteer" and he gave a description to the F.B.I.

It matched mine completely.

I was relived to know that I was not insane and they had a good description and face to hunt for now. Vince is going to college to be a schizophrenic specialist. He is going to help with cases and work as freelance. I am sure he will be good at it. It is good that he was recognized for his talents.

* * *

In the days afterward, I had a hard time sleeping. Who could blame me? I took the pills Dr. Coller told me about and was sleeping on my own by the fourth day.

I guess I was really tired, the first night I didn't wake up for fourteen hours. It was wonderful.

* * *

We pulled up to the hospital where my dad slept. I took five steps out of the taxi and paused.

Sidney stopped and looked back at me, "What is it?"

I counted these steps every time, ever since the accident, and every time, on my return, backward. "It is nothing honey. I am sorry let's get going." I did not count another step.

We got to his floor and a smile flew over my face. I was going to tell my dad the good news. The station was going to promote me. Starting Monday I was going to be Detective Jayson Pinc. Just like him.

Sidney stopped about halfway down the hall. "I will give you your space. I love you, honey. Go tell him the good news." Her face was tearing up. I could not tell if it was joy from my promotion or if it was my father. She hated to see me like this.

I saw the door. I did not count a single step here. I was so proud of myself. I took a deep breath and put my hand firmly on the door. I pushed and felt a slight resistance and a metallic clang flew into my ears.

I remember flying back with tremendous force and feeling my body being hurled into the far wall. Smoke and fire poured out of the room.

The oxygen rich environment of the hospital made the fire burn fast and hot. The fire took over the hall and then, like a scorpion stinging itself. The fire ate all the oxygen and died in seconds.

I could feel my face was burned, I didn't care. "DAD! NOOOO!"

I stood and ran into the still burning hot room. Through the smoke I saw him. His body was torn to ribbons. Blood splattered on the wall and fire crept up the chair I always sat in. I fell to the ground and put my head on his bed. It was hot and smelled like ash. I could not stand if I wanted to.

I looked up and saw the wall, door side. There was something written buried under the soot.

"No cops! You just lost another string. We will play again very soon."

It was signed. "Puppeteer"

That was the worst day of my life.

After the Fact

Some things I am still completely in the dark about. Such as, how did he make my phone ring without it making it show up on recent calls? The only thing I could come up with is that he must have used a short wave radio to direct the frequency to my phone.

But I have tried to make one and had little to no luck. Where did he get my prints?

All the questions may be answered someday but for now I guess they remain a mystery.

There are so many things that are surging through my head. Someday, I will get them all out and make the "Outlet" my therapist wants. But for now, I really need some sleep.

Till next time I speak to you. "Good night."

Made in the USA
Monee, IL
20 October 2021